FAMILY PLANNING

KARAN MAHAJAN was born in 1984 and grew up in New Delhi, India. His first novel, *Family Planning*, won the Joseph Henry Jackson Award and was a finalist for the Dylan Thomas Prize. It was published in nine countries. His second novel, *The Association of Small Bombs*, is on the list of TIME's Best Books of the Year 2016.

Praise for *Family Planning*

"Mahajan's real success lies in his brutally honest unpacking of Delhi ... a knowing, deeply felt portrait of a Third World city at the beginning of 21st century ... [A] blend of the farcical and the thought-provoking that would count as ambitious for writers far more experienced."

—***Biblio***

"[A] delicious satire."

—***The Indian Express***

"An attention-grabbing debut written at a furious pace ... at once absurd and moving."

—***Deccan Herald***

"Mahajan has an eye for the ridiculous and an ear for comic dialogue that bear him out well ... the farce never seems forced, the domestic chaos is well-etched and the humour is deadpan and unselfconscious – a rare enough quality in Indian writing ... a relief from the spate of navel-gazing first novels we've been subjected to."

—***Mint/The Wall Street Journal***

"[As] close to life as possible ... Karan Mahajan's *Family Planning* is smart and funny. Pick it up."

—***Mail Today***

"From the loaded title through the shenanigans of our political netas, Karan Mahajan manages to weave a readable tale with sarcasm and wit ... It is a most promising start. I have no doubt we will hear more about him in the years to come."

—***Khushwant Singh***

"[E]xtremely comic, and one of the cleverest Indian satires in recent years ... a realistic look at contemporary Delhi ... a fantastic debut."

—*Elle India*

"Brave, breakneck, and amusing ... Irreverent, fresh, and sometimes, given its author's youth, preternaturally wise ... Almost every page bears a passage worth quoting."

—*The San Francisco Chronicle*

"Mahajan's sprightly first novel portrays India's capital – 10 million strong – in all its explosive fecundity ... Mahajan is only 24 years old, but has already developed an irresistible voice with a rich sense of humor fueled by sorrow."

—Ron Charles, The Washington Post Book World

"A spot-on satire of Indian family life, globalization and intergenerational strife."

—*The New York Post*

"An excellent debut ... A portrait of family that is both comical and heartbreaking ... Mahajan's effortless blending of comedy and tragedy is irresistible."

—*Publishers Weekly*

"Sharply written, bracingly funny, and unexpectedly moving – Karan Mahajan combines 'take no prisoners' satire with haunting insights into the human condition."

—Manil Suri, author of ***The Death of Vishnu***

"The truest portrait of modern New Delhi I've read, and the funniest book of the year."

—Suketu Mehta, ***The Daily Beast***

"Comic novels, full of loveable eccentrics and sly social commentary, seem to be one of 'new' India's main exports; this is one of the sharpest and funniest examples."

—***The Times*, London**

"Mahajan ... has a mature and impressive grasp of poignant comedy and has opened up Delhi to western readers in a way that a more overtly politicised novel may not."

—***The Observer*, London**

"Readers of this New Delhi-set comedy of manners are in for a treat ... Mahajan, with supreme self-assurance, fashions a subtle, cutting take on modern India."

—***The Guardian***

"Charming and hilarious."

—***Elle Magazine*, "Hot 20: The Best in Art, Film, TV, Music and Books for 2009"**

"Mahajan's debut is sharp, funny and stylishly assured. Hugely enjoyable."

—***The Daily Mail***

"Sure to pick up a huge readership ... [A] subversive, clever read set in India ... Laugh-out-loud anarchy with echoes of Philip Roth's Portnoy's *Complaint*."

—***Red Magazine*, "Top 3 Must Read Books" (UK)**

"[A] bittersweet comedy set in a thoroughly 21st-century subcontinent."

—***The Financial Times***

Family Planning

• A Novel •

KARAN MAHAJAN

HarperCollins *Publishers* India

First published in paperback in India in 2016 by
HarperCollins *Publishers* India

Building 10, Tower A, 4th Floor, DLF Cyber City, Phase II,
Gurugram Haryana – 122002, India
www.harpercollins.co.in

P-ISBN: 978-93-5264-197-0
E-ISBN: 978-93-5264-198-7

2 4 6 8 10 9 7 5 3 1

Designed by Sarah Maya Gubkin

Printed and bound at
MicroPrints India, New Delhi

For my loving parents,
Veena Mahajan and Gautam Mahajan

CHAPTER I

QUESTION HOUR

OBVIOUSLY, MR. AHUJA—Minister of Urban Development—couldn't tell his son that he was only attracted to Mrs. Ahuja when she was pregnant. That he liked the smooth, alien bulge of her stomach or the tripled heartbeat when they made love, silently, shifting over each other. That the faint fetal heartbeat ran under the speeding pulses of man and wife, calming him, holding him back from instant climax. Or even more fantastically, how, at times, he could imagine the unborn eyes of the fetus watching him, pleading for another sibling—begging, sobbing, moaning through the parched throat of his wife . . .

It was morning and Mr. Ahuja waited at the bus stop with

his eldest son, Arjun. The sun swung over Delhi like a fiery wrecking ball, the entire city exploding with mirages and reflections that hurt the eye, Marutis and Toyotas and Ambassadors glittering by at top speed in their metallic finery. Clouds heaping in cumulus shelves overhead. The chalky pavements dizzying under eddies of dust. At least Mr. Ahuja was in the shade, under a tree, with Arjun. The middle-aged minister was becoming hard of hearing—the traffic on Modi Estate Road came to him like the indistinct whirr of a waterfall—but oh yes, he *had* heard Arjun's question. And the question was *Papa, I don't understand—why do you and Mama keep having babies?*

The boy had been as discreet as the bus stop would allow. He had waited for his other siblings—Rita, Sahil, Rahul, Varun, Tanya, Aneesha, Rishi—to leave. And then he had walked up to his Papa (Papa who insisted on seeing off the eight of his thirteen children who attended school every morning) and popped the question with the abruptness of a coin-toss in a cricket match. The words were said—Arjun turned away jauntily, thrust his fingers into his torn pockets, and scratched his hairy thigh. His white school pants were too short; they rode up around his ankles.

Now, both Mr. Ahuja and Arjun saw the Delhi Transport Corporation school bus floating on a cool mirage of leaking oil and blazing road. Time was running out.

In the end, all things considered, Mr. Ahuja decided he could not let the bus win. So he said, "Son, I told you about the Yograj Commission findings, correct? Then? You know I'm not a fanatic, but findings were hundred percent clear. We need more Hindus in India."

"So I'm—we're—just a political cause for you?" asked Arjun, twisting his neck to peer sidelong at his father.

"No, son. But you know how it is—these Muslims have so many wives, and their families keep growing, and what are we Hindus—"

"Do you even know my name?" Arjun asked.

"Son!"

With a tragic swing of the schoolbag, Arjun boarded the bus and was gone.

The bus accelerated heavily onto the road. The children leaned into the aisles; their water bottles swung in the air, briefly unanchored, sloshing. As Arjun scanned the lolling heads for a seat, he wished he had learned to mutter under his breath *(Goddamn politicians want goddamn Hindus goddamn fuck fuck)*. Then again, the skill was practically useless in his house where even the most regular conversation with his half-deaf Papa was—*to Papa*—a muttering under the breath. What luck, though: the only vacant seat was next to Aarti. She was a girl from the neighboring Convent of Jesus and Mary—a girl he liked enough to brave the usual heckling that burst from the back of the bus when he talked to a girl, even though he was sixteen. Today, the hecklers seemed hungover. Aarti closed the *Pradeep's Physics Guide* she was reading and they began talking. They talked about this, that, Bryan Adams, this, that, Bryan Adams's evergreen classic "Summer of '69," wasn't he wonderfully throaty, had she seen the new Bombay concert video, and what about that superb line when he said "Standing at your Mama's porch you told me it'd last forever it was the summer the summer of '69," what was he talking about, his lost childhood or his gained virility?

But really, Arjun wished he could tell her how he hated the daily morning bus-stop ritual, all eight kids trooped out onto the sidewalk by a man who couldn't hear anything, the eight kids now splitting into opposing factions and groups with the fickleness of politicians—each faction a campaign of shrill voices and stupid triumphs such as determining who could chuck Rita's water-bottle farthest across the road without cracking the windshield of a car—and all this ridiculous brouhaha expiring the minute the buses arrived and dragged the kicking, screaming mobs away. But the family was not a mob. The family was a solar system. The family had planets and satellites and the occasional baby that burned its way in like a mewling meteorite. As the oldest child by four years (the other children were separated by only nine to twelve months in age), Arjun had by now played every role in this evolving system: Pluto, the Sun, Jupiter, everything but a satellite, really. He replaced Mama as head-honcho when he was thirteen and she was recuperating from a difficult pregnancy, ten kids orbiting around him, tripping over their laces to get a piece of him, waiting for him to proclaim judgment on the crooked fixture of their ties—and now? Now he was Pluto again, cold, on the periphery, unimportant. He still had to read nursery rhymes to the four babies and soothe his pregnant mother by whistling filmi tunes, but otherwise he was trapped with twenty-four other probing eyes spinning around him—eyes that saw him only as a big threat to their personal nutrition at the dinner table.

Arjun was the biggest and ate the most. He had no privacy in the house and hated that. For instance: last night, for exactly 1.67 seconds, at 23:35 hours Indian Standard Time he had walked in on his parents doing it in the nursery. There in the cleft between the three cribs on the pinkish floor lay Mama on her back in a polka-dotted nighty, Papa bubbling uncertainly beyond her huge stomach, the papery jaws of his pajamas famished around his ankles. The four babies in their cribs were screaming; Mr. Ahuja twisted his head in panic; Arjun stumbled back into the corridor. The impression he retained was less a photograph and more a rash: the negative of his own skin blazed and exposed. Immediately, he was crazed with questions. How did Mama and Papa still have sex? How did their two lumpy bodies stack up, each one lost in the vast, flabby expanse of the other's skin?

Was this sex or—swimming?

He'd always imagined they had sex when all the children were at school.

Maybe they did, thought Arjun. Maybe they were at it again.

The thought annoyed him, and as revenge on his parents, he told Aarti on the bus: "Speaking of which—did I ever tell you about my band? We recently covered Bryan Adams songs. B-side sort of stuff, you know?"

"Really?" she asked.

"Yaah. You should come and watch us!"

They passed over a series of flyovers, and the driver heroically hastened the ancient bus down the slopes. These overpasses were Papa's concrete humps, Arjun realized. Flyovers were being constructed all over Delhi as part of Urban Development Minister Ahuja's plans to rid the city of traffic lights and reinvigorate traffic flow: even now, a number of flyovers lay incomplete, their two rising slopes frozen in midair like tongues that failed to touch.

He wondered what tongue on tongue felt like.

"I'd love to," said Aarti.

They arrived at school. "See you later, okay, bye!" he said, swiveling his heels toward the gates of St. Columba's, and she said nothing, only looked him in the eye, and that was a good sign, Arjun wanted to slap himself on the back, God, she was so pretty! With her slightly upturned nose and the way she pretended to be so interested in everything you said, the two dilating pools of her eyes so large and brown and patient! How she sat most days in the bus with her hair listing on her left shoulder, a notebook pushed out at right angles to ensure Arjun maximum readability (she liked playing noughts and crosses, Flame, Hangman, unabashed vestiges of junior school), the pen poised in his direction like a microphone, her bra strap straining through the tight fabric of her shirt—man. Her glances were like doodles—swift, often harmless, and entirely charming; every configuration of those eyebrows, mostly jesting, could distract Arjun from the distinguished antics of afternoon traffic. He feasted daily on her handwriting. He liked the sheer *fatness* of it. The sharp blue ink electrified around bulbs of white space. He could go for a spin in those letters.

But now the giant cross of the chapel loomed over him. He suddenly wished he hadn't lied to her about the rock band. But it had seemed like a good idea at the time. And, he supposed, it was the one thing his spying parents and siblings didn't know about him.

He was a rock star.

CHAPTER 2

MR. AHUJA'S RATHER UNMANAGEABLE SECRET

ARJUN WAS LOATH TO ADMIT IT, but he had his father to thank for the extended flirtation. The construction of flyovers had landmarked the city with pillars of rubble and rusty MEN AT WORK signs and mesmerizing shivers of arrow-sharp steel pointing skyward; a bus ride of eight minutes now took a wondrous fifteen. But Delhi believed itself to be crawling out of a chrysalis. The Super Prime Minister had declared a genocidal war on traffic lights. The opening of flyovers was second only in excitement to India-Pakistan cricket matches. Commuters bravely accepted the temporary congestion and looming phallic shadows as collateral for development.

Only Mr. Ahuja and a handful of his juniors at the Ministry of Urban Development knew they were wrong.

Delhi, quite simply, was fucked.

Mr. Ahuja rapped the teak table in the study with his knuckles. The beautifully detailed paper model of the Flyover Fast-Track, New Delhi, Circa 2018 vibrated, and a few dinky cars crashed off the model flyovers onto the cardboard pavements below.

The room sounded hollow. Mr. Ahuja felt unbearably lonely in his study. The mechanics of the whole thing were vaguely amusing: no matter how deaf you were, you could hear the dull plunk of hollowness. His awkward "encounter" with Arjun in the nursery last night and then at the bus stop in the morning had left his stomach feeling raw. All through his walk back home, he'd wished he could talk to the boy. The loneliness only compounded his problems because his first impulse when he felt at all uneasy was to plunge himself into the midst of a crowd, to feel the flitting glances cleanse him like the random water-jets of a sprinkler, and right now there was no crowd to speak of, only the giant expanse of the study, the pinnacle of his career hardening before him in teak wall panels and carpeted floors—empty. He hated emptiness. He hated it here in his study and he hated it in his office. He was never happier than when he was at the helm of his colossal domestic factory—loading the children into his Toyota Qualis and driving them to India Gate for a midnight ice cream, watching twenty-odd eyes affix to the prized fruit hanging on a tree in an orchard, feeling the hot cluster of their bodies behind his back like a small army—all to the dismay of his bodyguards who were supposed to shelter him from crowds. His two bodyguards had no work. They had stopped accompanying him to the office in his second year. Now he grieved for their absence. He grieved that he had given them up—that assiduous pair of Balwant Singh and Ram Lal—to a shabby domesticity, that he had let them become *maids* in the house, washing and drying the truckloads of dirty clothes the children shed daily with the alacrity of porno stars. Sometimes you could see the two men sitting beside a large slab of marble at the back of the house, on their haunches, smoking bidis, flogging pairs of wet jeans against the rock, and the sight would arouse sympathy in Mr. Ahuja. At these moments, he would feel the temptation to embezzle ministerial funds for a washing machine—a temptation that flared upward from his groin and culminated in a facial grimace, but no, he never gave in. He knew this: Mrs. Ahuja was *obsessed* with washing. If he ever bought a machine, she would end up staring at its window all day, hypnotized by the knots of clothes unfurling under curtains of detergent.

Wasn't it like that with TV already?

At least the TV was in the nursery where she could also watch over the children.

Mr. Ahuja needed to change channels. He lay back in his chair, hunched forward, and coughed violently into his red silk tie. The act was comforting: the silk tie was the only object of clothing that escaped Mrs. Ahuja's washing and *therefore* defined him, breeding and sustaining a microcosm of smells and germs and saliva (he often fell asleep in his office in the weeks after a difficult campaign) that he'd encountered over his long and varied career as a politician. The tie featured a repeated pattern of cricketers playing straight drives. He coughed again into the cricketer closest to himself, rolling up the tie as if to dam in the germs. He loved the tie; it drew him from his introspection, he could smell it and be whisked to a better time. The tie was his most loyal companion, his pendulous sycophant, his brief reprieve from the lazy, flowing kurta-pajamas that he'd started wearing ever since he became a politician. But he loved the tie mainly because it was a birthday present from his first wife, Rashmi. Rashmi: Arjun's mother, dead. No one ever spoke of Rashmi in his household, and how could they?

Arjun didn't even know he was Rashmi's son. None of the other children did either. Mr. Ahuja had done his best to keep this fact a secret.

Yet, today, when Arjun had taunted him at the bus stop, when Arjun had cheekily asked *Why do you and Mama keep having babies?* he'd wished to say *Are you aware that you didn't even walk in on your real mother last night?*

Luckily, he'd had the foresight to use Muslims as scape-goats.

In this he had become like all his colleagues in the party.

Now he simply felt dejected. Mr. Ahuja stood up and paced. His ratty Bata shoes plowed a soft ravine through the powdery blue carpet. He pressed the buzzer lying on the table with his pinky (his preferred weapon of choice for reprimanding and demanding) and walked over to the window. He saw his own reflection in the tinted glass and tried to ignore the sights of

Delhi that lay beyond his watery visage. His face was a succession of comforting curves; not a handsome face, but one that could appear perpetually interested, the brows raised on a pivot of white hair above his nose, the cheeks retracting into an intelligent angularity when he spoke, the eyes small and intense, yet not beady. Here was a man who could appear dire in his earnestness, a forty-three-year-old with a paunch whose face was still gaunt and young with stubble. He withdrew a little from the glass, holding his gaze. It had always amused him as a boy, that if you brought your face closer and closer to a glass, you would stop seeing your own reflection; eventually you'd be so close to your ghost in the polished surface that you could look through its eyes. And because you shared eyes, you couldn't see it. You could only see the city spread out ahead of you, a palimpsest for the cities to come, a teeming, fertile ground where one could sow concrete and watch it sprout into strange, often hideous shapes.

And what did one see when one was close to someone else's face, making love? What did one see beyond?

Mr. Ahuja knew: it depended completely on who you were making love to. With Rashmi he had seen nothing beyond—just a blackness, a black cricket field full of black cricketers, the four towering stadium lights blessing every cricketer with not one, not two, but *four* shadows; each cricketer appearing, from a height, like a tiny wad of flesh affixed to the center of a shadowy quadrupronged compass, and then he and she would be standing high above the field and the lights would go off one by one and then they were alone, circling above the pitch black, together. The cricketers would disappear. The compasses would disappear. There'd be nowhere else he'd rather be.

And with Sangita—perpetually pregnant, constantly fertile Sangita?

Sangita with her still-peculiar odor of mothballs and Tiger Balm? With her body oiled from the constant attentions of the massage-wali? With her thick left hand always pressed against the small of her back? Her old-person groans? Her almond-milk breath? Her chin acne? Her belly button upturned proudly? Her stomach fabulous and fragile, all at once?

Yes. That was the problem. With Sangita, you couldn't get past the details.

Worse, Mr. Ahuja had never really tried. But thinking of Sangita had turned him on, and in a sudden rejuvenation of passion, he exited the study, walked to the nursery, knocked on the door, and entered.

The nursery was a large whitewashed room with ten cots—three of which were full at present (Vikram: two months, Gita and Sonali: eleven months)—and the permanent fixture of Mrs. Ahuja sitting in the center on a stool, knitting. She was forty years old—the type of forty that led people to comment "You look too young to be sixty." Her head was covered with a dupatta and she looked up for a brief instant. She was tall and had an imposing bun of black hair. She always wore gray saris during the day. The matronly cloth revealed a sideways curve of stomach cleavage. Streaks of silver hair fell across her face; her mouth was tightened into a hyphen in the manner of a woman who is terrified of her own luscious lips (only she had tiny, thin lips). A fan creaked overhead; the actor Amitabh Bachan muttered imprecations from the TV.

The TV was placed in front of the window, an alternative natural light. Mrs. Ahuja hated natural light. The room smelled of saliva and Johnson & Johnson baby powder.

Immediately Mr. Ahuja started bellowing. "What was Arjun doing here last night? Why was he coming here, tell me? I thought I told you he doesn't need to look after the babies. He's a grown man now—he shouldn't be jumping from his bed the minute a baby makes a noise, correct? Are you listening?"

He hadn't initially intended to bellow. He'd meant to get on his knees before her and whisper inanities into the smooth rotunda of her stomach. But being back in the nursery, he'd been struck afresh by how perfectly horrible it must have been for his son to stumble upon his parents sprawled out on the floor, and his thoughts sputtered into puffs of irritation. He was his dark, bitter self again. He saw the reality of the situation in the form of a newspaper headline: MINISTER AHUJA PROPOSES NEW BILL FOR SEX EDUCATION ON THE *FLOOR* OF THE *HOUSE*; BABIES TO BE *EXPOSED* AT YOUNGEST AGE POSSIBLE.

"I am listening, ji," said Mrs. Ahuja.

Mrs. Ahuja did not raise her voice, partly out of habit, partly out of resignation, mostly on purpose.

Mr. Ahuja, not hearing, continued. "Accha. Also, tell Shanti I want her to make me khichdi to take to office. I need to eat light food for lunch. Everyday these buggers at functions make me eat bloody heavy Kashmiri-type food."

"Ji, Shanti has left."

"Where has she gone?" Mr. Ahuja scowled. Then, in a graceful arc from irritation to affection, he lifted up baby Vikram and started cooing.

"Home, where else?" said Mrs. Ahuja, casting off a stitch from her needles.

"Why did she leave so suddenly?"

Mrs. Ahuja mumbled, "She threw away the towels."

"So she was *fired*?"

"Yes, ji."

Mr. Ahuja sighed. He put Vikram back in his crib and tickled his stomach. Then he turned to Mrs. Ahuja. "Darling, what is this you've done? Please explain this to me. What crime has she committed against you? Sangita, it is because of women like you that the servant-types will one day have a union. Whenever you feel like you fire them. Then you make my son do the work instead. You've made Arjun into a maid."

"The maid is not listening," Mrs. Ahuja offered. "Today she tried to throw the towels I keep in the almirah."

"Arjun did this?"

"She, ji."

"She who?" Mr. Ahuja threw up both hands.

"The maid."

"You and your pronouns. Which one is this now?"

"Shanti."

"I thought she was fired."

"She is," said Mrs. Ahuja. "Because of towels—"

"Hai Ram, Sangita. I've seen those towels. They're completely ruined. They're moth-eaten. They're rough. They *should be* thrown away."

"Okay, ji," said Mrs. Ahuja, rocking a little on her bamboo stool. "I was only trying to maintain the hygiene. You only said we needed the hygiene."

"HYGIENE?" coughed Mr. Ahuja.

"Ji, when I am going to do toilet, after I have used mug sometimes there is still some cleaning required on buttocks. For that I am using towels. Hygienic it is—"

"How many times have I told you: you don't DO THE TOILET? You GO TO THE BATHROOM!"

"Sorry—"

"What sorry, Sangita?" said Mr. Ahuja. "My children are all speaking like you now. Please. Firstly, either speak Hindi or speak English. This in-between thing is stupid. None of this nonsense. Get rid of the towels. Bring the maid back. I don't have time for this. And I thought I told you to throw these away," he said, pointing to the oranges that sat on the windowsill. "These oranges—look at them, Sangita—they are all green. That is mold. That is bad for these babies breathing. Do you know that? Already all of them have asthma? Please, no more trying to save on these things."

"Okay, ji," she said. She wiped her hands on a napkin. A pyramid of scrunched napkins lay on the plate behind her. "I'll give them to Shankar's family."

Shankar was their servant. Miraculously, he'd been their servant for a decade. All the other servants—and as a minister,

Mr. Ahuja could have had an entourage of domestics—were dismissed within days of their hiring.

Mr. Ahuja intervened. "Do no such thing. And please—I don't want Arjun to do anything today. No diaper changing, no massage, no baby exercises. I need to talk to him today."

"Okay, ji," she said.

Then, hesitating, she gestured toward the household deity—the TV—and said, "He died."

"ENH?"

"He died," she said in Hindi. "Wo mar gaya."

"*Tomorrow, kya?* Eh?" he said. "Sangita, why would I say *tomorrow* when I am saying *today*? I want to talk to him today!"

Mrs. Ahuja gave up.

CHAPTER 3

THE SUDDEN BRIDE

WHAT COULD HE TELL HIS SON? Mr. Rakesh Ahuja wondered.

Son, these things are normal in a family? Your mother loves babies and wants more and more? People have sex in this manner all the time—how else is it done in villages? Ahem, what exactly is a condom?

He reclined in the back seat of his official Ambassador car, hypnotized by the driver's constant and incoherent grumblings about a recent cricket match. He was on his way to work. His sense of sudden well-being was reinforced, no doubt, by the serenity of Delhi at 7:50 A.M. before 10 million people woke up, had their morning tea, and decided, in a mind-boggling coincidence, that *today* they would put their all into bringing the city within inches of utter ruin. The city's roads at this hour—actually about the same temperature as just-burnt toast—looked cool and shady through the tinted glass. On the central island on the main road was an array of red pots with saplings that he hoped would bloom the year Rita—his second favorite after Arjun—turned seventeen, and he followed the island with his eyes till it disappeared under the largest permanent shadow in Delhi, the underside of the Secretariat Flyover, the most beautiful, complex sandstone monument this side of Rashtrapati Bhavan—its four arms and blossoming ventricles of greenery and the general curvature of the roads designed to look like a giant lotus from the air, so that when Mr. Ahuja rolled down the window he could feel in his dry throat the concentration and densification of life that the flyover would bring to the area when it opened three months from now.

He secretly relished the fact that the space under flyovers provided housing for shanties and beggars and runaway children and the homeless; he liked that you could grab the yellow railing and walk alongside the traffic, a thing unheard of in India; he saw the bowed columns and arches that held the entire structure aloft and was conscious of having recolonized the city.

He was glad he had a city to save him from his personal embarrassment.

No—he was glad the city hadn't yet collapsed.

He needed to discuss Rashmi with Arjun before he himself was subsumed by political problems. He'd been postponing the inevitable discussion for years, but today he'd almost barked the secret out at his son. This wouldn't do: a proper father-son talk was needed.

Mr. Ahuja closed his eyes as the car varoomed under the overpass, its belly sculpted like the chassis of a 747. Two wings of foliage dropped on either side; cool, corrosive dampness fumigated the car. Then they were out, and Mr. Ahuja was looking up and over his shoulder. A banner attached to the front of the flyover was fluttering precariously in the wind and asking a poignant question about AIDS, which actually turned out to be a poignant way of advertising the quiz-show *Who Will Win One Crore Rupees?*

Everything about that first marriage to Rashmi had been plagued by contradictions—his initial wise-assed refusal to have an arranged marriage (he had shaggy hair and razor-sharp sideburns and an IIT degree in those days), his parents' coy compromise ("Well, see some girls, you don't have to marry them") and his final defeat (marriage). He had chosen defeat. Rashmi was beautiful, a wispy Punjabi girl with cheeks that seemed curiously drawn in, and a nose that cast a perfect shadow on her upper lip. He saw her in his own house, both sets of parents looking on sheepishly as the boy and girl interacted mechanically and formally. After they left, he told his parents: "No, there's no way I am going to have this nonsense arranged marriage." He knew he was breaking their hearts; they were ailing, they wanted to see him settled. But he had pledged revenge on his parents and he couldn't remember why—wasn't it because they themselves had had an awful married life, because they had sent him away to boarding school, because their constant fighting had made him feel so insignificant, so ignored as a child?

Later that day, however, he stooped over the gray, unwieldy phone in the verandah and listened for footsteps. Then he circled the phone. He cut wide arcs, then smaller arcs. Momentarily, he leaned against the bookshelf, whistling. Finally he swooped down on the damn thing and called Rashmi and asked her on a date and they went on a date and they went on many dates thereafter (all unknown to the four sheepish parents)—Rakesh gingerly holding her hand during the screening of *Sharaabi*; Rashmi leading him to a secret spot in Humayun's tomb where they kissed over the musty coffin of a dead Mughal courtier; both ducking into the old communist haunts of Connaught Place and smoking cigarettes. He loved her for her indignation, her anger at the way New Delhi's colonial airs distracted from the actuality of its massive slums—and her unwillingness to let that make her bitter or sad. She was the most earnest person he knew, and something of that earnestness played against his own sense of tragic irony, of rejection, and bloomed into romance.

No one knew of this romance, least of all his parents who had given up hope for their son. To them, Rakesh appeared to be losing his mind. He had just finished his four years at the Indian Institute of Technology in Delhi, earned a bachelor of science degree (with distinction!) in civil engineering—the most marriageable and marketable degree of his time—and now he wanted to do what? He wanted to enter the Indian

Administrative Service, the IAS. The unimaginable: he wanted to shed the world of logical remuneration that had been planned for him, play the intellectual lottery of the civil service, become a *babu*. He wanted to shape cities, be a servant of the Public Works Department. Rakesh's parents thought they had lost everything, and the exhaustion of keeping their only child on track as he veered away from them would have killed them if he hadn't come in one day and said: "MamaPapa. I want to marry Rashmi."

He told them everything. His own revenge had failed him.

Rashmi and Rakesh were married. The marriage had many highlights, yet nothing filled Rakesh with greater elation than sitting on the faux-throne during his wedding reception and having relative after relative come and pay obeisance (and cash, of course) to the stunning married couple. He liked sitting on the dais and hooking visitors with his eyes and then watching them proceed to greet him. It was a benign, harmless science, and yet—it required skill, to maneuver people, to engineer their fates in a way that was best for everyone. That was true engineering. Days later, he entered the room for the Administrative Service exam like a conqueror, smirking at the invigilator. But sitting at the desk, a married man, no longer a virgin, all he had were dreams of grandeur, images of gaunt architects poring over drafts of New Delhi and Chandigarh—his feet pattering alongside Rashmi's through the perfect city. He was so in love that he failed the exam.

Now, academically thwarted, he sent last-minute, desperate

applications to American colleges. He was accepted by the BR Institute in Vermont for a PhD in civil engineering. It wasn't the best program but he went anyway. Rashmi enrolled in a journalism program at the same school and Rakesh acquainted himself with the vast boredom of suburbia and the glimmering perfection of American design. He disliked America; he felt self-conscious being the only Indian in a hundred-mile radius; he wished he could be back among Delhi's teeming millions. Even Rashmi, comfortable in any setting, felt lonely. And then, deep into their first white winter, their longing for India exaggerated, both unable to handle the desiccation of central heating, Rakesh joked, "It's too cold in this country to do it with a condom."

Nine months later they had Arjun.

Arjun changed everything. If before Rakesh had felt obligated to stay in America (he wanted to prove to his father that he was responsible), in Arjun he found the perfect reason to return home—didn't they want their son to be Indian? Didn't his grandparents want a part in bringing him up? How would Rashmi cope on her own? But, surprisingly, Rashmi was the one who wanted to stay. She wanted clean air for her son (Delhi had made her asthmatic), safe roads, crisp winters, an idyllic American childhood. Rakesh told her there was no such thing—that she enjoyed being an exotic foreigner too much. Immediately he felt bad. Immediately she reminded him that if it weren't for him, they'd never have moved.

"I'm going for a drive," she added.

They'd been arguing all day.

"Look, I'm sorry."

"There's no point being sorry," Rashmi said. "You've ruined the day. It's the one beautiful Sunday we've had in months and it's ruined. You want complete control. If you don't get it, you're like a child. You start snapping."

"You're right. I'm sorry. I shouldn't have said that. You're not exotic at all. You're a *homely convent educated girl with B.A. and fair and lovely skin*."

"Rakesh!"

"I'm only joking, darling!"

"I'm only going for a drive."

Rakesh held her playfully at the door. "Look. The babysitter's here. What will I do? What is a man to do in such a situation? How should a man in the twentieth century keep himself busy while his baby is sat?"

She laughed. "You should propose to her and take her back to India. She's fairer than I am. Your mom and dad will be pleased."

Eventually, after much cajoling, he made a deal with her that he be allowed to sit in the car as well, and Rashmi agreed on the condition that they wouldn't exchange a word the entire time—if she went shopping in the mall, he'd shiver and quake in the parking lot with his hands thrust into his pockets; if she pulled into a gas station, he'd not be the least bit chivalrous and would in no situation offer to fill up the car and would instead fiddle with the knobs of the stereo like a distracted boy. Rakesh agreed to all these ridiculous terms because he'd always feared the worst from Rashmi's angry solitary drives (she was willful but absentminded), and he felt better, as the object of her rage, being by her side.

"You're too much, Rakesh," she said. They'd been silent for a good twenty minutes and were slowing down by the mall.

"I know. I know," he said. Then he grinned. "So are you."

He also knew this was the end of the argument: she lay her hand on his; she had forgiven him; they were quits. Then Rashmi parallel-parked the car in a tight space on the narrow road with breathtaking skill and stepped out of the vehicle on the side of traffic and in doing so found herself in the direct path of a motorcyclist who had careened the wrong way down a one-way street; and with that, Rakesh's time in America was over. The motorcyclist slammed straight into her and carried off in a whirling agglomeration not only Rashmi and three-fourths of the open door and a stack of magazines crammed into the driver-pouch but also managed to tilt (in the manner of water pushing open a sluice) the parked car away from the pavement so that Rakesh, who was stepping out from the passenger's side at that very moment, was whooshed onto the ground, his head stunned by debris, his left eardrum punctured by a flake of glass, his palms bloodied by savage, cold concrete. The sun overhead was gorgeous and blinding and Rakesh sat up on the pavement and waited for someone or something to strike him down as well. Nothing happened; no one came for him. He was already struck down. The sun was maddening. For two hours he could make out nothing in the left ear, then the doctors worked a minor miracle and left him tolerably deaf.

About Rashmi, though, nothing could be done. She had died on the spot.

It would be incorrect to say Rakesh stopped functioning: if anything, relatives said he took the death very well, as best he could have—what else could the poor boy do? He disavowed America and all the promise it supposedly represented (the motorcyclist had died, too, a month later, never waking from his coma) and flew back to India with his son. He started living with his parents again in their cavernous Greater Kailash house, Arjun left to the devices of his grandmother while Rakesh brimmed with rage and hurled himself into politics with a newfound fervor. He knew it wasn't his parents' fault that he had fallen in love with Rashmi, even if they had introduced them—but he blamed them nevertheless. He blamed them for his disastrous temperament. He blamed them for the sharp tongue that sent Rashmi shooting out the door and into the car. He blamed them for their inhospitality and bad cooking, for not keeping a home in India that would have tempted Rashmi to return. He blamed them for their legacy of bad luck that wasn't bad enough: Why else had he survived?

Worse, he worried that his son's life, Arjun's life, would also be ruined by his mother's disastrous ineptitude at child rearing: hadn't she produced one failure already?

So, when his parents suggested a second marriage and Rakesh said yes, he did it with the irony and bitterness of a man who didn't care. He did it because he was enraged that his parents could suggest remarriage this soon and because he wanted to spite them by marrying someone absolutely inappropriate. He did it for three-year-old Arjun. He did it because he wanted to be a politician, and politicians need wives. He refused to let his parents be the slightest bit involved and decided to go through the motions—the perusal of the classified ads, the screening of the bride-to-be, the uneasy conversations with the girl's parents, the slightly ashamed call for dowry—purely for personal entertainment. But the girl was pretty, and personal entertainment soon gave way to a more primal lust when he drove to Dalhousie (alone) to see her. It was a traditional upper-class Himachali-landowner household—the food served on shiny silver platters—and he watched the girl carry nothing but her reflection on such a platter as she was ushered into the drawing room by her father. He ogled the tight curve of the girl's breasts pushing up against the sari, the tautness of her exposed navel, the small coins of her ears.

To his parents, he only handed a wedding card.

"You've become American," they said. "You're only having one function. What will all your relatives think? We have to invite them. Please let us invite them. We've never heard of a son who won't make us meet the bride before he's married. You haven't even shown us a picture of Asha. Don't disgrace us."

"Is that all you care about? *Your* disgrace? You waited only one month after Rashmi died to start telling me I should get remarried. Now I'm getting remarried. Just be happy."

All the weeks till the wedding, he'd rise early in the morning to masturbate in the bathroom.

On the wedding day, though, seated next to him in the tent, minutes before they circled the fire, was a different girl, an ugly girl, a girl whose skin was coarse and whose features seemed to have been molded lazily from a single piece of dough, all flat and asymmetrical and stubborn, a toothy embarrassed smile on her face. He hadn't noticed her face at first because it was obscured by various danglings of gold; then she quickly lifted her veil and frowned at him. Rakesh was utterly dazed. He thought: *What if it is the same girl? But without makeup? How can I hurt her feelings?* But no, she clearly wasn't the same girl. This girl had no breasts. Rakesh knew he could have gotten up then, that moment, and put an end to the whole farce, he could have stood in the middle of the tent and kicked over the flames with the elegance of an enraged filmstar and asked no one in particular: *What kind of nonsense is this?* But he didn't. Instead, Rakesh felt the eyes of his parents upon him—the layers of talcum powder shivering hideously on their skin like unlicked salt—and knew immediately that he would have to go through with the marriage.

After all, wasn't he getting married to *spite* them? Would his mother and father really believe this was a different girl? Or would they think Rakesh had simply lost his cool at the last minute, reneging on the only real decision he'd made against their wishes?

He looked at the girl's parents for a reaction—*Were they her parents?* The father was slouched eagerly with a hand massaging his knee; the mother was sitting up straight, her back against a pillar. Rakesh was overwhelmed by curiosity. Who *was* this new girl, this sudden bride? How did she and her "parents" think they could possibly get away with this? Did they really think he'd marry her and *stay* with her? Did they have a stable of divorce lawyers lined up to suck him dry after the wedding night?

Were they not aware that the Ahujas were a very powerful clan?

Now he felt at ease. He could marry this girl and immediately divorce her. He could claim the marriage wasn't consummated. This was the benefit of a subdued and poorly attended wedding: you could treat it like a brief, perverse entertainment and no one else would know. He had felt the same way after Rashmi's death, when—to escape the smirks of seepage on the walls of his parent's house—he had taken to strolling through crowded marketplaces for the comfort of anonymity, ducking through a maze of bodies. But soon he realized that his face drew people's attention. There was something about the pleasant calculus of muscle and gravity and tension accumulated beneath the surface of his skin that attracted both sexes and he began to enjoy their looks, their looks not of envy but a sort of buried awe, an unconscious empathy. He began to long for that empathy. He began to alter his expressions to arouse that empathy. He began to perform for *himself*. Rakesh and the girl circled the flames and were married.

CHAPTER 4

DEMOCRACY ROCKS

IN SCHOOL, Arjun was mercifully distracted from thinking about his parents' sex life. He was a rock star; that was his revelation; he shared it with his friend Ravi. The words themselves were somewhat humbler: "Dude yaar, let's start a band. I'm getting a total feeling yaar. Want to blow some amps, man."

Ravi said, "Did I tell you what happened to me yesterday?"

This was a typical Ravi response. He was a stooping, sardonic-looking boy with wide shoulders. He was shaped like a coffin. He scratched his atrocious wild stubble when he talked and he liked to talk: something crazy was always happening to Ravi.

Arjun listened as Ravi narrated an unlikely story involving his father's new Hyundai Santro, a monkey, and a dog.

"Then?" asked Arjun.

"Then I ran over the dog and honked at the monkey."

Another Ravi theme: emerging victorious.

"Cool. Want to be in a band?"

"Okay," he said.

"Good. I'm—"

"Let's clear up some fine points first. Are we going to be an alt-rock, alt-country, indie, electro, electroclash, raprock, hard rock, or metal band?"

Ravi was obsessed with details and planning. He had found a way to turn this to his advantage. For example, he started studying for exams months before they were scheduled, thus ensuring that he was relaxed and could even get in a few games of tennis the week before the exams began; Arjun hated that. He also came first in school, always had; Arjun hated that too. On top of this he was an excellent drummer. He practiced and practiced and practiced till he sounded spontaneous.

"We'll play rock, man. Fucking rock," said Arjun.

"Yaar. This fucking rock only exists in your fucking mind."

"Hard rock yaar. Hard fucking rock."

Even this was not enough for Ravi. "Okay. Seventies' hard rock, like Rolling Stones, or eighties' rock like Springsteen, or nineties' rock like Oasis—"

"Rock like your mother."

"That makes no sense," Ravi said. "Explain that to me."

"Oye shut up—"

Ravi laughed. "Okay. Let's do this band thing. I'll put this on my U.S. college applications. Harvard will eat it up. You know Natalie Portman checks all the applications."

Together they approached Anurag and Deepak in the break period.

They were far less responsive. "A band? Who's going to study for the exams? Your dad? We don't all have connections to get us passed," said Deepak with a broad grin.

"Oye—listen at least yaar," said Arjun. "I'm not just starting a band for bloody time-pass. My dad said, if we want, we can perform at the Indraprastha Flyover inauguration. Next month it's happening. I thought I'd ask you first. If you say no, no problem. I only asked you because you have no other friends except me. I thought, yaar, if you guys aren't in a band, how will you pick up babes?"

"Interesting," drawled Deepak. "So now you're pursuing charitable work, is it? And uncle just happened to say, okay son, I want you in a band? He's finally realized you're a duffer in all other departments?"

Anurag said, "Duffer in all other departments!"

Anurag was Deepak's sidekick.

Deepak said, "Also, tell me, is your Ministerji Papa still milking your Mama's you-know-what for Parliament? Is he trying to be the *father of the nation*, ho-ho?"

He helpfully put his right index finger through his left fist in slow, heaving motions. Arjun was used to this. Ravi, Deepak, and Anurag were united in the common goal of taunting Arjun about his massive family. They had nicknamed him Torn Condom—marking him as the first of a long line of contraceptive mishaps. And they thought he had *only six siblings*.

"No yaar, they are all Arjun's kids," said Anurag, slapping Deepak's back.

"You want me to slap you or what?" Arjun grimaced.

"Why don't you sing?" said Deepak. "It'll be the same as slapping."

Anurag snorted. "It'll be the same as slapping! Because your voice is like a slap!"

"You're truly mad, man," said Deepak to Anurag. "Do you have to say everything you think?"

Anurag shut up.

Arjun was onto bigger things. "We need a name."

Ravi said, "Three dudes and one duffer Arjun."

"That's a good band name."

"What about the Torn Condoms," suggested Deepak.

"You want me to slap you or what?" Arjun inquired.

"Best name ever!"

Things went smoothly from there on. Once a band begins debating its name, it is already a band. Of course, as the recess progressed, other, smaller, pettier debates were to follow. They had to. This is all essential if one is to start a band. Tension, violence, must exist on the surface. The band is about sublimation. For instance: at one point in the conversation, as they passed by the water cooler and Ravi explained in great detail the drum fills he had mastered, Arjun rocked on his heels with irritation and declared himself the lead singer.

It was a useful announcement. He didn't play any instruments.

For the rest of the school day (effecting an intelligent grin while Mr. Nath lectured about "the importance of finishing your class eleven course as soon as possible"), Arjun had flashes of last night—vivid, wondrous, hoary exposures. But what disturbed Arjun were not the flashbacks themselves but the fact that he *wanted* to imagine his parents, the same way he liked bringing his finger close to the blurred blades of a table-fan on his desk, inches away from understanding pain. This was his arrogance; he didn't try to forget what he had seen last night—no, he wanted to conjure it up and then *defeat* it with a vision of his own. If only Aarti would go from being a sexual fantasy to a sexual possibility, one vivid enough to walk with him into the memory-trap of the house, to lay beside him, to drown his parents' gasps with her own . . .

The afternoon bus ride exposed the silliness of his ideas. She wasn't that sort of girl. She was innocent and cute. She had a slight, adorable waddle to her walk as she came down the aisle of the bus. She had long drooping eyelids and an upturned nose that defied the downward gravity of her face. And what hair! Sexed in every direction! Arjun glanced at the hard knobs of her knees, then followed the spiral of scab lines upward, nodding his head as he finished sipping in the warm sheen of her thighs.

He thought she was heading for a seat at the back. Then the knees suddenly backtracked: she sat down next to him. Unbelievable.

"How do you get time to be in a band?" she asked, once the bus had departed. "I have no time for anything. I have the most boring life possible. I'm always studying for FIITJEE." FIITJEE was a coaching institute for hopeful applicants to the Indian Institute of Technology. "I come home from school in the bus. Then I eat lunch and watch *Happy Days* in half an hour, using *Happy Days'* ending to time the end of lunch. Sometimes I get time to shower, sometimes not. Then I take an auto to FIITJEE. I sit still for four hours. I take an auto home. The time by now is seven thirty. My physics tutor comes usually at seven forty. So I eat Maggi Noodles. Then I sit still for two hours. At ten I watch *Friends*. I hate my life."

One finger plucked away at the belt-loop of her skirt as she spoke. She was unconvincing. She seemed to Arjun to be proud of her own hardship and boredom. He responded in kind, and explained at great length how he had shown talent at a young age in singing and so his school principal made special concessions for him, letting him practice in the small auditorium during the morning assembly, saying, *Arjun you can skip extra classes; you have done so well in your exams*, and how when the principal's wife had died, he had asked Arjun and the band to play behind the funeral pyre so that the fire was between the principal and the band, and

Arjun said that was the only time he couldn't sing because his throat was full of tears and soot, but he had seen the principal singing his songs through the heat mirage of the pyre, the principal had made their music *his* (oh, you want to know why a Christian's wife was having a cremation, er, she was Hindu, yaah), but apart from that, the only time the band met was for three hours two times a week. Otherwise, he was studying, studying, studying, he also wanted to get into IIT. His Papa was an IITian—see there was all this pressure, could she understand?

Apparently she did. She gravely nodded and said, "When is your concert?"

What did he look like to her? he wondered. Was his hair sleekly angled so as to cover his massive forehead? Had she noticed the way his nose was ribbed in the center?

He said, "No set date yet."

Aarti looked crushed that he hadn't mentioned a date she could have mulled over, considered, and then denied with an explanation of how busy she was.

Now it was her turn to be silent.

"When are you free?" he asked.

She scrunched up her eyes and thought and thought and thought. "Sundays only." Then she added, "And even then I am busy sometimes. My Dadi is very religious and we have to go to the mandir and do this puja for three hours. I can't tell you how boring it is, yaar. First, we sit on the floor and the pandit brings samagri and oil. Then we recite Om Bhur Bhava Swaha fifty-five times. I believe in God, but do I have to say it fifty-five times? So yaah. Even on Sundays sometimes I am with my family."

"So what?" said Arjun. "You can bring your Dadi and your Mama and your Papa—whoever. The concert will be part of a flyover opening. My dad is a minister."

"Your dad's a minister?"

"Not corrupt, I swear. So far, I think I'm the only one taking any kickbacks in the family."

This was his standard line for girls.

"You mean?"

"Football team," he said. (He wasn't on the football team.)

She laughed. "What's your dad's name?"

"Rakesh Ahuja. He's the Minister of Urban Development." He quickly added, "He wasn't involved in the Gujarat riots."

"No, no, I'm sure."

"Yes. And he hates Yograj. You know? Yograj Commission. The guy who caused the Gujarat riots."

"Accha," she said. He could tell she appreciated his openness. She continued. "I hate him too. When the riots happened, I wanted for the first time to be a politician, yaar. I thought this is really too much. In this day and age for this to happen. But everyone makes fun of me for being idealistic. Also, you cannot enter politics without time and connections. I have neither—"

Marry me! thought Arjun. *Marry me!*

Then the bus braked and he strode past her and stepped off the goddamn bus into the divine and dehydrating afternoon light.

• • •

Now all he needed was to organize a concert. On a Sunday. He walked home with growing excitement. He'd talk to his brothers and sisters. He couldn't tell them what he had seen last night in the nursery, obviously not: firstly, it was disgusting, and secondly, people have sex all the time in this country, doing it in fields and huts and buses and naalis and even in servants' quarters when your master was shouting "Raamu, please get the chai," and you ignored him because you were thinking, "Oh! How nice would it be to have one billion and *five* children in this country as opposed to one billion and *four*!" and it really wasn't something he could describe.

But he could tell them: *Listen, I am in a band.*

He could gather them in the backyard and say: *Okay, it's a little more complicated: I am in a band with three dudes to impress a girl.*

He could run his hands through the thickening tuft of his hair and say: *Listen, if I help you with trigonometry homework, will you come watch my band play and bring five of your friends along, preferably female since you go to the co-ed schools and females are the biggest fans of male-made rock music? Remember, five times eight is forty, which is how many people will attend my concert if you help me, and is also proof that I can help with maths! And if you say no, then I will tell Mama and Papa that you (Varun) smashed the window of the Ambassador, and that Rishi broke . . .*

Yes. He'd organize a concert in Aarti's honor. He walked home through lashings of dust.

CHAPTER 5

MR. AHUJA RESIGNS

Mr. Ahuja, meanwhile, was resigning in Arjun's honor.

Making a decision to resign was easy enough: Mr. Ahuja had done so sixty-two times in his career. He'd learned early on that in a lethargic political system—racked with sluggish subcommittees, idle parliaments, and five-year promises—the fastest way to get one's own government to take action was to throw a massive tantrum. To hand in one's "papers." To complain to the press.

The breakdown of his resignations was roughly as follows:

Over irritations caused by colleagues in the Flyover Fast-Track: 37

Over being offered a share of a corrupt deal: 15

Over anti-Muslim legislation (such as renaming streets in Delhi so as to have distribution of Muslim and Hindu names proportional to the respective populations, or the establishment of a Hindu Holocaust Museum that declared that nearly 10 million Hindus had been massacred by Muslim invaders): 6

Over *not* being offered a share of a corrupt deal (these were those rare deals where every single member of the party was involved—why should he have been left out? Didn't he have thirteen children to educate?): 2

Over snide remarks directed at him about family planning: 2

What would happen after he sent in his letter was routine. He'd take a day off from work. He'd ignore phone calls and refuse to clear files. The Super Prime Minister—Mrs. Rupa Bhalla—would call him up and say, *What is the matter?* Then, when Rakesh explained, she'd cajole and weep and invite him to dinner and request him to stay. Let's reach a compromise, she'd say. He'd decline. She'd beg, the small knot of her hands quivering on her gargantuan thigh. He'd be terrified. He'd stay. It was crucial that everything have the clap-till-you-drop predictability of an encore at a concert.

More often that not, the problem was fixed.

Now Rakesh sat in his office at the Ministry of Urban Development and fiddled with the ragged papier-mâché box that contained his sixty-two letter-headed missives. This was the first time he was actively searching for a *reason* to resign. He simply wanted the day free to talk to Arjun.

He pressed his buzzer.

There was a cough behind him. Mr. Ahuja turned around.

Sunil Kumar, answerer of buzzes, token drone of the bureaucratic beehive, purveyor of chai: Sunil Kumar stood before Mr. Ahuja in a perfect, diligent slouch.

"Bring me chai," said Mr. Ahuja.

"Yes, sir. Also, there is a file for you from the Ministry of Minorities."

Then he disappeared. After a few minutes, he returned, sans chai.

"The file?" Mr. Ahuja asked Sunil Kumar, staring out the window.

"The file is in your office only."

Sunil Kumar was shouting but neither Mr. Ahuja nor he noticed. Years of working together had guaranteed them an equivalent deafness.

"It is not here, yaar. Otherwise I wouldn't call you," Mr. Ahuja said, speaking into the glass. It was suddenly as if he were at a huge rally—perched upon a pedestal four stories high, suave and sage-like in a giant, bulletproof box. The only flaw in the design was that the audience happened to be inside the box with him. He couldn't be saved.

"Sir, you are looking sad," Sunil said. "Besides, it is bad when the nose of a great man is touching the window, no?"

"What?"

"Sir, are you seeing that bird on your table?" He pointed

to a small curio on Mr. Ahuja's table, a tiny silver bird reposing perilously, almost magically, on the sharp tip of its beak—the remainder of the torso suspended in air like a seesaw waiting to drop. "Well sir, the nose is a great man's *center of gravity* as well. And so sir if you are pushing against the window, then perhaps it is showing some deeper sadness."

"You talk such nonsense. Are you trying to be a poet like Vajpayee? Now give the file."

"Which file?" Sunil asked.

"You just said you had given it to me. Now you're asking which file?"

"Sir—"

"The file from the Ministry of Minorities!" Mr. Ahuja yelled, turning around now. His nose felt sufficiently frozen.

"Oh sir."

"What?" Mr. Ahuja asked. *"What?"*

"It is under the bird's beak only."

It was. He knifed open the envelope with his thin index finger and took out a poorly cyclostyled one-page document. It was a bill entitled *Diversity of the Motherland Act*. The bill, buttery in his hands, paper-cut thin, see-through in the muted light, to be voted on ten days from now, was a pernicious almost-fascist document, calling for the compulsory registration of all Muslims "for reasons of diversity and national security"—a document Mr. Ahuja recognized because he had so vehemently opposed it at the cabinet meeting two weeks ago.

The author? Vineet Yograj. The head of the infamous, eponymous Yograj Commission.

Perfect. This was all he needed. Vineet Yograj was his nemesis.

Mr. Ahuja usually dictated his letters on the move, but today he sat down at his desk and rattled away at his keyboard.

Dearest Shrimati Rupa-ji:

I hope this finds you in the best of health and wealth. I decided to write to you in the eleventh hour about our fellow party member Vineet Yograj—a man towards whom I harbour, if you recall, the same level of affection I feel for the Pakistani cricket team, George Bush, and the advent of the tiny triangular wedge of hair grown by men between the age of twenty-one and thirty-one under their lower lips. I apologise in advance for ranting; more is to follow; in the course of this letter I may well resign; heaven help us if I do.

Etc. Etc.

Firstly, I would like to address the Diversity of the Motherland Act. I am so moved by this communal anti-Muslim document that as a companion I suggest the following—A bill to legalise betting over the outcome (i.e., death toll) and frequency (i.e., when) of Hindu-Muslim communal riots in India and to achieve this by allowing for the trading of Riot Stocks. Let us call this the Riot Stock Exchange Bill. If we are going to kill people, let us at least make money off it!

(Enclosed)

On the subject of money, three days ago I discovered that the Honourable Secretary Vineet Yograj had harnessed the loose morals of several key individuals in the Urban Ministry using chains made of gold and was awarding contracts for flyovers to the DharmaLok Company, run, as you are aware, by his son-in-law Vir Pranam Bakshi, former alleged rapist. The DharmaLok Company is best known for its exquisitely substandard materials, gross overcharging of the Ministry and a standard rate of dividing the surplus "funds" between good members of the PWD (20%) and Vineet Yograj's family (80%). Worse, it seems that I have acquired such a reputation for honesty and associated evangelism that Yograj didn't even see fit to offer me the standard Ministerial share of 5% (I am joking, of course!). If he had, I would of course have taken the black-money and not come true on my end of the bargain. Furthermore, I would have been able to intervene before my wonderful Cabinet Secretary for Urban Development added a full twenty-five extra flyovers for the corridor near Rohini—two to be constructed over primary schools, three over Heart Institutes, and one over a—yes—another flyover (this is not Shanghai!).

Of course, there is also the problem of Yograj's social behaviour, which, I must admit, as a long-standing member of this party, I find disturbing. When not engaged in petty corruption that could ruin the future of an entire city—the country's capital, that too—he is well occupied by the pursuit of making a complete and utter ass of him-

self at social gatherings, on TV shows, and at weddings. His favourite and most detestable move is to introduce himself as the "Hony. Secretary" of the party. "Hony" not "Honorary." You will be surprised how many people know the English word for randiness that I am covertly referring to; one MP from a province of U.P. who is good friends with Yograj and who I will not name was the first to point it out. I think it is unfortunate that the whole country is having a hearty laugh at the expense of one of our spokespeople.

Then there is the issue of the Grandfatherly Peck he was found giving to children under the age of five. No additional description by me can further fertilize the field day the newspapers had.

Finally, are you aware that he has brought about a motion to change the symbol of the party?

(The original party image for the KJSZP[H2O2] Party was a bar of soap with an inverted, spiky bottle-cap pressed under it. The image was one of cleanliness, improvisation, urban thrift—of keeping your soap elevated above the sink so as to prevent it from slowly dissolving away at the point of contact. Unfortunately, during the Kargil War, it was discovered, in a random survey, that most people simply thought the contraption was an overturned, defeated battle-tank. Further, because wars in India generated universal patriotism—there was no question of being peace-mongers for Pakistan—volunteers for the party over the years had been taught to stick posters upside-down, keeping the tank erect. Ready for firing as it rolled about on its soapy wheels.)

The new symbol he is suggesting is a flyover with a cow stationed under it. Not only is this a personal affront to me, but it is also a major misunderstanding of our goals: one, we do not want to encourage cows to seek any kind of housing—whether temporary or permanent—under flyovers, and two, has Mr. Yograj forgotten that nearly 80% of this country lives in the villages and has never seen this much vaunted flyover?

The point, quite simply, is that Yograj is not a countryman.

Worse, Yograj is not a party-man.

Which is why I will not tolerate Yograj's presence in the party one more minute. I do hope you will take the needful action; it is long overdue; I have asked you before. This should be a fairly straightforward process. I have clear proof that Vineet Yograj has interfered in the Flyover Fast-Track Project. Therefore, I am hardly out-of-line in asking that action be taken against him. Indeed, I am ready to give up everything for this cause.

For instance, my Minister-ship.

Please accept my resignation.

Your Humble Servant,

Rakesh Ahuja.

Something had happened in the writing: Rakesh felt transformed. His vital signs were skyrocketing. He slapped his blue chair into a violent swirl and watched it dervish to a stop. He knew his resignation letter to the Super Prime Minister (SPM) had gotten out of hand. His rage had edited out everything but the most forthright expressions of rudeness (*I do hope you will take the needful action; it is long overdue; I have asked you before*). Just like frowning itself can generate sadness in a person (rather than vice versa), the act of resignation had flexed Mr. Ahuja's latent musculature of revenge, heightening his sense of disgust not only with Yograj but also with the SPM, Rupa Bhalla. Yes, it was *she* Rakesh was most disappointed in—Yograj was scum, he expected nothing better from him—but the SPM had encouraged his more idealistic tendencies and then stood by as his Flyover Fast-Track was summarily junked.

When she'd come to power, she'd given him his portfolio of choice—the Ministry of Urban Development—and routinely congratulated him for running a "tight ship." Rakesh too was overjoyed, foolishly energetic, puffing up his chest on his stupid tight ship. He had spent years studying sustainable design as a hobby, and his suppressed civil engineering knowledge had thrummed out in straight, thick, confident lines from the left-brain when he came to power.

He was unusual in that respect: a minister who actually had a skill-set that rivaled that of the engineers doing his bidding. In his first months, down in the mosquito-haunted basement of the PWD building, he had laid out the Delhi

Master Plan, smoothed the predictably yellow document with two formless, coral-trapping paperweights, and superimposed his vision on it with the lightest of 2B pencils. This was his bid to defeat fifty years of slipshod Delhi Development Authority planning with one grand gesture; he transferred all the civil servants that argued with him; he bullied his witty Under Secretary into excavating the secrets of the ancient bureaucracy. He greeted truant employees with giant pay-cuts. He threatened to resign when needled with political interferences. The newspapers and magazines—*India Today*, *The Times of India*, *The Hindu*—all those publications that hoped for a great, intellectual, middle-class hero, trumpeted his virtues. For them, the suave black-haired minister was the new Lutyens. He was an antidote to the sleepy ninety-year-olds who ran Parliament. He wore a suit and tie and had an IIT degree and was proficient with e-mails and the Internet and had an American brashness about him that made him seem like a holdover from Rajiv Gandhi's technocratic cabinet—only with bigger, better brains. He certainly had a plan. He wasn't waiting for the forced trigger of an Olympics or Asian Games to get the city stenciled into shape. He wasn't stacking half-hearted terraces of tar over the city for temporary respite. He was building a system that seemed positively futuristic, a brilliant aside to the National Highway he was also implementing. Tracks of elevated road adding extra brio to the tired Ring Roads. Gurgaon and Noida brought within twenty minutes of IIT campus by a miracle. Squat malls zoned in the space left free beneath the cacophonous, if numbingly constant, roar of traffic on the flyovers.

Individually taken, each flyover was a work of architectural genius (shaped like tigers, elephants, bicycles, and even a rhino), built at such an unusual elevation that beneath it one could create tiny cities—malls and gardens and fairs massively shadowed by concrete.

Reality was the ultimate bulldozer. Political pressures and jokers like Yograj had contorted the plan into a shape that was far from perfect. The paper model in Rakesh's study at home presented a severely shrunken idea of the problems that awaited Delhi. Yes, traffic would be eased, but too many flyovers were being erected, the city was being randomly suffocated with concrete, the horizon had collapsed under a view of second-floor balconies and clotheslines fluttering with underwear, every politician in Delhi wished to distract his disappointed voters with a giant, noisy, jing-bang of modernity, the flyover. For some reason, no one doubted the sandstone sexiness of an overpass. People believed in them with a preindustrial innocence. They earnestly put up with months of noise and pollution if it meant fast transit in the future.

Only, of course, transit wouldn't be much faster. It'd just be an uglier city.

Now Rakesh bitterly perused the e-mail. He'd suppressed his disappointment over the Flyover Fast-Track because he knew that idealism itself was a sort of political immaturity. Sending in such a fiery resignation would curtail his chances of advancement in the party. The SPM would not tolerate such blatant rudeness. She was more goddess than woman. It was a ritual in the party to drink the rosewater she'd used to clean her feet. During cabinet-shuffle-time ministers and MPs pitched tents in her garden to stress their loyalties. So what if the party was at an all-time low. So what if it was losing all the state polls and its popularity rating was dismal. He ought to soften his language. He ought to remember that this e-mail was written *specifically* with Arjun in mind. . . .

What the hell—he pressed SEND.

"Darling, I've resigned," he said to Sangita on the phone. "Tell the children I'll be coming home for lunch. But don't tell them I've resigned, obviously. You know how they become when I tell them. They will want to know everything. Then they'll cry. You've raised true drama queens."

"Okay, ji."

Mrs. Ahuja was blasé. She had good reason to be.

Mr. Ahuja put down the phone, his head spinning. There was the question of what he would say to Arjun about Rashmi. For a decade, Rashmi had been receding from his memory. She had become a swirl in the sink, a hot-blue flame that appeared on a gas stove, the smell of a tissue as it took away ribbons of snot, the static in someone else's cell phone, a pencil of memories sharpened into nothing. Words: *Darling*, *Kanjeevaram*, *Tragic Eyes*. But last night, his pajama drawstrings dangling down in a huge comic bow, Rakesh had needed her *body*. He had needed her entire being to be transposed swiftly beside him—hologrammed over and around Sangita's pregnant form, a dose of beauty to undo his embarrassment—but she was gone. And it was Arjun's fault that he had had this revelation. It was Arjun's unawareness that killed Rashmi once and for all.

CHAPTER 6

WHO DIED?

ARJUN WAS SECRETLY PLEASED to hear from the guard that his father was coming home for lunch. This meant a later meal and more time to organize the concert. He kicked off his shoes and watched the insoles pop on the front verandah of the house. The house—12 Modi Estate—was a squat bungalow that always smelled of the rainy season, its many awnings and verandahs making it a haven for loiterers, right-hand men, chamchas, servants, maids, shawl-sellers, bored bodyguards; Arjun walked past the walkie-talkie wielding lot.

The door of the house opened into a massive wind tunnel of fans and gray floors. The drawing room was congested with kids—its horrible maroon color scheme gave it the aspect of a dingy beauty parlor. Neither Mama nor Papa had good taste, Arjun realized. They had no interest in decoration. Instead, a flood of giving had besieged the Ahujas since Mr. Ahuja made minister, and the house had been furnished with favors—the mismatched sofas and oddball paintings and the giant statue of a naked British boy in the front saying more about the taste of the givers rather than the takers. Because, as Arjun knew, his Papa took everything. He was blissfully indiscriminate. Eventually, he begged these favor-seekers for fungible essentials, and so baby products and creams and clothes came pouring in like predated dowry. The toys and clothes for the older children Mr. Ahuja made a point to donate to slum-dwellers so his brood could stay clear of being spoiled—*they are at high risk of becoming brats*, he'd told Arjun. Of course, he made his children do the giving; giant feasts were organized in the back garden where local sweepers and workers were ladled food from five giant containers by the Ahuja children—an Ahuja meal on a larger scale, basically.

Arjun wondered if Mr. Ahuja wanted babies only so he could eat away at the endless supply of gifts and sweets and food.

He found the theory highly plausible.

He was humming a song and washing his hands in the bathroom when Mama knocked on the door, peered in, and said, "Have you seen? He died."

Then she left. Was this her way of apologizing for last

night? Arjun finished swilling the water and watched himself in the mirror as he spat white foam. Everyone always said he looked like his father, but today he was all Sangita, the handsome pimple on his forehead like a bindi, his lips loose and sullen. He was almost amused by the idea of his mother being a sexual being: he'd taken for granted that the number of children his Mama and Papa had was equal to, if not more than, the number of times they'd had sexual intercourse (they had twins). Last night, then, completely shattered the part of him that'd been taught—mainly by America—that sex was the spontaneous transfer of fluids between very attractive, naked, blond people. Clearly, Mama and Papa were (still!) horny for each other. Clearly, their sardonic disinterest in each other was repressed magnetism. Clearly, last night he'd walked in on an act of passion.

This, against all odds, he could learn to respect.

Now the question that remained—the question that could alter completely his idea of how many years it was possible to lead a double life, to lie, to get away with risks that came with a certified *Adult* license—was this: Who was the horny one? Mama or Papa?

He spat out a phlegmy jet into the sink.

Arjun found Sangita sitting glumly in the nursery with a newspaper. She was wearing her stiff gray sari.

"He died," she said, offering no context. "He was here one minute and then—phut—just like that, gone."

"Oh no, I'm so sorry, Mama," said Arjun, looking sad. "I don't think I knew—him. Who was it?"

"Such a nice man he was. Gave tea-shee to his workers for no reason. Used to donate so much to the charities. All the tires you see the poor boys on the road playing with, he gave them. Such few nice men these days."

"I'm sorry to hear that," said Arjun. "When is the cremation?"

She said, "What cremation, bhai, they don't even give him the honor of that these days, such little time."

"He was a Muslim?"

"Arre, why so many questions? Are you not watching? How can he be Muslim and going to the temple for charity? Do you know any Muslims who give to charity?"

"No," Arjun admitted.

"And do you know of a Muslim woman who runs a company?"

"Was he murdered?" asked Arjun. "Usually if the cause of death is unknown then they need the body and do tests to see . . ."

"He died because of using cell-o-phone in the tub," she said, sighing. "But it was not his fault, naa. They killed him."

"*They?* Was this in the papers?"

"Zee-TV, naah, who else."

Arjun was dumbfounded. He returned to his room.

• • •

Rita was giggling in the hallway. "Yaar, it's Mohan Bedi from *The Vengeful Daughter-in-Law*. I think his contract finished, so they, you know, killed him off. He was everyone's favorite, so God knows why they killed him. *So* nice, *so* charming, *so* elegant, *so* handsome, *so* fair, *so* talented, *so* husband-y, *chho* chweet . . ."

CHAPTER 7

QUID PRO QUO

ARJUN SHOULD HAVE KNOWN this is how he would make peace with Mama—offering condolences for the death of a TV character. Having done the needful, he was ready to ask his siblings for a favor. A favor about the concert. This was no easy task, Arjun knew. Firstly, it was two thirty on a weekday, a time of hunger; Papa would be home soon. Secondly, the house was a calamity in suspension. The house was the riots of 1947, the children massacring one another with a calm disrespect for personal boundaries. Or, at other times, as Mama liked to say, the house was the Agra Mad House. Or as Papa liked to qualify: on fire. No amount of analogizing or eulogizing could suffice, however. A family of thirteen in modern-day India was a disaster, a game of marbles that had lost its marbles, a giddy *Titanic* aching for its eventual iceberg, a pack of wolves with no Mowgli to raise, a team of jihadis so bored they'd declared holy war on one another.

As Mama had one day said, "What are these Americans constantly complaining about, every day here is a September 11 only!"

She had said, or shouted, this with special reference to a series of kamikaze paper-planes that had struck the warring pixels of the TV screen one bright Sunday morning, disrupting the eight o'clock Bhajans Sangita liked to watch.

Varun, his hands still nimble from wing-folding, screamed from the drawing room, "MAMA, SAHIL CALLED YOU OSAMAMA!"

But Sahil was innocent and sitting silently. On a sofa. In pajamas. With a fried egg on his lap. Which was not supposed to be in his lap but rather on a plate that was now fallen on the ground.

Sahil screamed, "MAMA, I DIDN'T! SHANKAR, GET THE TOWEL! VARUN IS MOCKING ME!"

Tanya put aside her *Harry Potter* and intervened. "Arre, Varun what has Sahil done to you? Why are you bullying him?"

Varun was indignant. "He called Mama a bad name."

"But he didn't," Tanya yawned. "*You* did."

"You said Mama's Osama!" said Sahil, furiously dabbing his egg-soaked knee with a piece of toast and slurping up the yolk.

Varun wasn't impressed. "So? It's funny, no? When have you ever cracked a joke?"

"But Varun—I mean, bhaiya—" Bhaiya was the respectful term for elder brother.

"You called me *Varun*?" Varun thundered. "Is my name Varun or *Bhaiya*? What, you see this?" This referred to Varun's balled fist. Of course.

And so Sahil learned. He had not flown the planes but he had to take the blame. The family was run on a system of mafioso respect, a constant tangle of snakes and ladders where the older you were, the longer you could rattle your tail and shake up the kiddies shinnying up the stepping-stool of experience. But being a wily old snake also had its disadvantages. It meant you couldn't ask for favors without coiling around yourself, tying yourself into a knot that could take years to disentangle.

Arjun understood that asking for a favor would mean years of sibling servitude, a debt that would be paid out in tiny pounds of flesh—flesh that was completely unnecessary since, ostensibly, one had the same flesh as one's siblings. And that is what made it so much worse. It was flesh for flesh's sake.

But a family shouldn't be run on a system of favors, an earnest voice inside Arjun said. *Everyone should favor everyone.*

What a delusion! The only time such delusions were even remotely true was on Diwali or Holi or Rakhi or Indo-Pak cricket matches, festivals that were contingent on the collective. For a day, each enmity or plot of revenge would be buried and a terrifying fealty would take over. Terrifying because it was so vicious. *You hit my brother with a water balloon? Well,*

I hit you with ten thousand! You buy a ten-thousand-explosions firecracker to scare my little sister? I throw a water balloon on it too*! Plus! Plus I buy a one-trillion firecracker, one that you will hear till the day you die!*

Arjun was a part of this family too. He knew how it worked and he knew he would encounter resistance, rubbing the match-head of his request against the rough responses of his siblings. Each one would require a separate strategy of appeasement. For instance, he would have to forgive Varun for his transgressions, his reckless cricketing in the backyard and the gulley behind the house. The austere shape of a cricket ball whizzing through the air would cause a gallop of heartbeats in the Ahuja household. And, occasionally, the cracking of a windshield. But Arjun had caught Varun at his worst, most humbling moment—when he had smashed the ball straight into Shankar the servant's brand-new Atlas bicycle, rupturing the spokes of its back wheel. The poor servant had wept, not knowing the cause of the damage. He had bought the bicycle with his own money (he had insisted to Rakesh that he wanted to be self-made) and was looking forward to cycling on it with his cell-phone cocked against his ear (this he had accepted from Rakesh on the condition that he would pay off the cost of the phone with cuts from his salary). But now the wheel would crack like a rib each time he perched on the seat. Varun had been characteristically cruel to cover up his misdoing. Each time he saw Shankar's five-foot frame hunched over the wheel, he would say, "What? You've started thinking of yourself as Gandhi-ji spinning the wheel or what?

Are you going to make clothes from it by sitting there only?"

Varun didn't know that Arjun had witnessed the entire event from the window, that Arjun had given Shankar money for the repair from his own pocket-money. Shankar had refused. "I'll get the sister-fucker who did this. He thinks he can come outside the minister's house and smash up his bicycle."

One morning, at the bus stop, Arjun finally told Varun what he'd seen.

"So what? He's a servant," Varun said.

"Yaar, listen to yourself speak before you utter words," Arjun reprimanded him. "You want me to tell Papa? Or worse, I can tell Shankar, and he'll enthusiastically fill your school water-bottle every night with liters of his spit. Or cut his nails in your mango milkshake. Just stop hitting the cricket ball blindly around the house, okay? Restrict yourself to straight drives for a week, see how it feels."

"With all due respect, Mr. Judge, Judge *Bhaiya*, if you will, maybe you are saying all this because you're, ahem, bad at cricket? What about all the times you made Shankar play badminton with you when he hates doing it?"

"Okay, Varun, that's it. I'm asking you not to be cruel to a person who has less money than you do, that's all, but now you leave me with no choice."

"No—" cowered Varun.

"Yes. From now on—" said Arjun.

"No, you know I—" Varun begged.

But Arjun was adamant. "From now on, you're going to have to play cricket with a tennis ball instead."

A tennis ball was for sissies. Thus, Varun had been emasculated. But even that was better than having Papa tell him he couldn't play cricket at all. That's how afraid he was of Papa (Papa, who rarely got angry but, when he did, could brainwash the entire household against you), even he, Varun, a man's man who popped the collar of his Modern School shirt to hide the giant yo-yo of his Adam's apple.

Now, Arjun knew, Varun would no doubt ask for a revocation of his softball sentence. He would claim he missed the sound of willow on cork, the fantastic wooden vibration of the bat passing through your whole body, stopping your heart for an instant.

Which he did: Arjun relented.

The same was true for the other children, with the exception of Rishi. Rishi's response to the generally bad-tempered tactics of his siblings had been to strike back with apology. He had been so thoroughly bullied by Varun, Rahul, Tanya, Rita and, yes, even the supposedly benign Arjun, that he sought refuge in the cool English lilt of the word *sorry*.

A typical Rishi sentence went something like this: "Sor-ry. Sorry. Sorry. Swaaareee. Swaaaaari."

And then, when you thought it was over, he would deploy his masterstroke, the sorry flurry: "I'm sorry."

"Okay, okay, fine, shut up, shut up!"

"Sorry sorry."

"It's time for dinner you bloody fool!"

They would head to the table. "Sorry sorry sorry but I'm really sorry, bhaiya, so sorry please pass me a chappati sorry sorry sorry sorry sorry—"

"What are you doing, son?" Rakesh would ask.

"Sorry Papa sorry sorry sorry sorry sorry sorry sorry . . ."

"Eh? What's he saying, Arjun?"

"Papa he's saying sorry sorry sorry sorry sorry sorry—"

"THAT'S THE SAME THING AS WHAT HE'S SAYING. SAY AGAIN?"

"I thought that's what you wanted to know—what he was saying?"

"Why isn't he bloody stopping! Son! Eh?"

"Papa, once again, let me repeat, RISHI AHUJA, YOUR SON, is saying: SORRY SORRY SORRY SORRY SORRY SORRY SORRY SORRY SORRY."

"Arjun, I'm sorry Papa's making you say what I'm saying. No, listen, I'm really sorry sorry sorry sorry. . . ."

With Rishi, it was call and response, you had to calibrate your tone so you didn't seem accusatory because if you did, heaven help your ears.

The rules of conversation in the house left little room for Arjun to beat about the bush. This Arjun knew: If you wanted to get a point across, you had to do it emphatically. There was little point in hiding your pain or expecting anyone to sense the subtleties of your personal torture. If you stared at your feet and circumlocuted, then another train of conversation would likely run right over you, flattening your putty resolve. You had to act fast and act quick and pretend, at all times, that the person you were talking to was (a) a person from the Agra Mad House, and (b) had been there for at least ten years, thus surviving electroshock therapy.

With Tanya—his sister who used her dark features to style herself into an emotional thunderbolt—Arjun expected sparks. "Why don't you ask Rita?" she would likely say. "She has so many friends." And, sadly, it was true. Rita and Tanya had nearly the same face—a pert button of a mouth set off against equine nostrils and baggy cheeks—yet Rita was fair and therefore pretty by default. Tanya reacted to this unfair favoritism by spending most of her time trapped in a dangerous circuit of personal toilette—applying makeup to cover her pimples even though the makeup only aggravated her pimples and caused her to apply more.

What she really needed, seven-year-old Sahil had one day

made the mistake of earnestly saying, *what she really needed was Fair and Lovely Cream.*

It was a rather large mistake. The family had felt that day not like a war zone but rather a bunker shaking under a war zone, everyone huddled together in a dense nest of limbs while the calamity happened overhead. A calamity called the perpetual wailing of Tanya.

Thus primed in the passions of Tanya, Arjun proceeded with caution.

"In a band, haan?" Tanya said, chewing gum. "What's it called? *I Failed Class Eleven?*"

Tanya was just discovering sarcasm, so Arjun let it pass. "It's called Radiohead," he said. Arjun didn't bother explaining that such a band already existed.

"Radiohead?" squealed Tanya.

"Radiohead!"

"Rahul," said Tanya, "Bhaiya's band is called Radiohead!"

"Bhaiya," said Rahul, dropping the GI Joes he was playing with. "Does this mean you'll wear a turban. Like a sardar."

Arjun glared at him.

But Rahul was full of questions. "Bhaiya, does your band have eighteen people?"

"Eighteen? Why?"

"Because you thought that under eighteen was not allowed for a rock show!"

"Good one, yaar," said Tanya, crushing slightly on Rahul's effeminate charms.

"I don't get it," Arjun said, even though he did.

"I do get it!" said Tanya, even though she didn't.

"Explain it to me, Tanya," said Arjun.

"Explain it to him," repeated Rahul.

"Why don't you explain it? It was your joke?" Tanya whimpered.

"So?" asked Rahul. "Bhaiya asked *you* first. Plus, I'm older and older wins. Right, bhaiya?"

This was typical, thought Arjun. Everyone was out to screw everyone else.

"Enough jokes! Now listen."

"Don't shout, Bhaiya," said Tanya, feeling ganged-up on, as she often did.

"Well, I want to ask you—and even you, Rahul—for your help. I want to have a concert for my band on next Sunday. I was wondering if you could bring a few friends to the house that day and ask them to watch my band play without laughing or criticizing?"

Arjun had expected the negotiations to temporarily break down at this stage, with Rahul and Tanya using their leverage to threaten inaction, to say "no," but instead they had just one bewildered response: "Why?"

Why, why, why? Why go to such lengths to court a woman? Exactly? Why not pause the lie where it was, let Aarti think you were in a band, ask her to come home, and not bother with the amateurish formality of actually playing? Why not just persist with the slow cadences of dialogue on the bus, win her with the tired complaining about school that drew people together on the ride home? Why not one day touch her hair as she thrust her head out of the bus window into the hot oven of the day? Feel a strand of her black shiny mane twanging between your fingers like a guitar string? And then know, gosh, this is nothing like a guitar string, this is not sharp or metallic or callous-inducing, why did I bother with *that* when I could have had *this* all along? Yes, why have a band and a concert and the dire hullabaloo of your brothers and sisters?

Was it because you were ashamed. Was it because the more you talked with the girl the more you were exposing yourself to scrutiny. You didn't want the girl to know that you were concentrating all your energies on the magnetic whirl of her eyes. You didn't want the girl to feel so special that she would then be superior to you, and therefore not want you at all. Even though she was superior to you: you who were just a liar praying not to be found out, a boy who invented a band to be special—for your sake, not Aarti's, if you had wanted her purely you would have leaped after her like an exposed wire, willing to face the risk of emotional electrocution. Not padded with the plastic of prevarication. These selfish lies.

"Don't tell anyone? Promise? I'm only telling you two. Don't tell anyone, okay? No, yaar, seriously? You swear on Mama? Okay. I want to impress a girl on my bus," Arjun told Rahul and Tanya. It wasn't a lie, but it wasn't the whole truth either. He wanted to be the center of attention, that was it, and it would be a huge added bonus if this attention included Aarti's rapt stare.

• • •

Arjun was shocked at the results. All his siblings obliged readily, making phone calls to their friends. The only other thing the children were so united in was their awe and admiration for their Papa, builder of flyovers, savior of constituents, handshaker of prime ministers and presidents, all of whom visited the house occasionally. Each child thought (and this would last only a short while, Arjun knew) that he or she was the only one who knew why Arjun bhaiya was having a concert. Each was touched that a person in a position of such power (the oldest! by four years!) would risk such vulnerability. After all, the prospect of girlfriends and boyfriends was usually treated with bouts of teasing in the Ahuja household. The teasing was a Newtonian phenomenon, an equal and opposite reaction to the taciturn way the children dealt with members of the other sex. If you didn't tell you had a girlfriend, and someone found out, well, then you deserved to be teased till you broke up with her, goddamn it!

Arjun's admission was different, though—more thoughtful, more mature, an unblemished secret worth sharing.

CHAPTER 8

FATNESS HAPPENED

RAKESH NEVER SHARED with anyone what happened on the night of his second marriage.

They had circled the fire, and then Rakesh had led the girl away and almost thrown her into the back of the waiting nuptial car. In the back seat, he stared at her angrily.

"I'm sorry. There's been a mistake," she said. "I should get out. I'm sorry, I was forced only. She forced me."

He interrupted, "Who the hell are you?"

She had a stirupped posture and a moon-shaped face and a muddy complexion and full cheeks and eyebrows that looked permanently raised and plucked. She looked like a black cat, in other words. Later, he realized this formulation was all wrong. There was nothing at all sly about her.

"Sorry, ji, I should leave," she said. "Sorry. Please. Let me leave only. Sorry." She was weeping now. The driver continued staring straight ahead, but Rakesh could see the muscles at the back of his neck throbbing; his brain was busy stenographing the gossip.

"Don't be dramatic," he shushed. "We are now married. You are my good wife. I am your good husband."

She understood. She smiled fakely and turned her head away and held up both arms and let the giant slinkies of her bangles slide down to her elbows. When they arrived at the hotel, she continued holding her arms up, as if Rakesh were prodding her forward with a gun.

In the hotel room he screamed at her. "Who the fuck are you?"

Her entire moon-face flinched and fluctuated, as if she expected him to slap her. "Ji, I am Asha's sister only," she said. "I am very sorry, truly. Please kick me out. I was forced. She forced me. Divorce me. I'll fall at your feet."

She fell at Rakesh's feet in a great din of gold.

"Don't be hysterical," he said. "Sit."

She sat down on the bed, cross-legged. She looked like a pagoda.

"You: What were you doing there?" he snarled. "Did you think—?" Then he started rattling off a long list of disgraces he would hurl upon her family. He'd divorce her. He'd spread rumors in Delhi high society. He had contacts in the newspaper. He'd sell the scandal to the *Times of India*. Of course they'd be biased toward him.

He realized that he himself was hysterical. To cover up, he said again, "Don't be hysterical."

"Sorry," she said. She looked bored. She bit her nails. Her eyebrows blessed her with a permanent look of condescension. This irked Rakesh, and she must have read this because she added, "Ji, please forgive. I didn't think that you—that you would finish the marriage only. I thought you would—"

"Never mind that," he snapped. "First you tell me. What the *fuck* were you doing there?"

She was silent.

"Okay fine. Do it your way—" He was pleased at how American he sounded. "Then let's at least have sex."

He thought this would get her to tell the story, but instead she complied. What type of trap was this? he wondered. What type of good Indian virgin complied so easily? Or maybe she was desperate to get rid of the heavy decorations of gold that she'd been sweating beneath? Regardless, he couldn't believe the nerve of the woman. Within seconds she sat naked, cross-legged before him. Only her impressive bangles remained bunched at her elbows.

He admired nothing. There was nothing in her body to admire.

He took off his clothes in a careless choreography: an

uninterested, you-leave-me-no-choice sort of way. His pants he kicked aside; the Nehru jacket slipped off with a flex of his shoulders.

But as he sat cross-legged before her, awkwardly, he couldn't achieve an erection. The girl and he looked like two naked people doing naked yoga; you could see it in the side mirror. The view of his failure made Rakesh doubly mad. If a woman was going to trick him, he thought, she might as well be attractive.

That was when Rakesh slapped her.

She started to cry again: he felt brutal, ugly, awful.

She was sobbing now in great malarial spasms; her jewelry was rustling and grinding like ancient machinery; she raised the back of her right hand to her eyes but the hand itself was trembling, ineffectual, and Rakesh watched with perverse fascination as her tongue shot out to divert the goo of tears and makeup and snot dripping down her face. Then he rescued her. He reached for her and pulled her down by her bare shoulders onto the bed. He lay next to her, stroking her hair. Both of them stared at the ceiling. In the side mirror it looked like Rakesh was dusting a jacket rather than stroking the black hair of his sudden bride.

This is the most awful thing I have done to a woman, he thought. I hope I am never forgiven for it.

He never hit her again. He whispered into her ear, "Now tell me."

"She forced me to wear her clothes and come to the tent. She is a very difficult woman. How can I explain it to you? How?" She was whimpering more than talking.

"Who is she?" he whispered gruffly. "Don't use pronouns."

"My mother, ji: She is not wanting any of us to get married. Yes, there are people like that in the world also. She wants all of us to grow old in her company. To be with her always. She is a hypochondriac and is always sick. She wants us all to take care of her till she passes away. But she will never die. A person as sick as her never dies."

She sat up and frizzed up her hair in what was a surprisingly mannish manner; fingers forking through from the front of the scalp to the back.

"For me, who am oldest and not so attractive, she always tried to find a boy who was *too* good-looking. This meant that no boy said yes to me. I got used to this. I thought I would not get married ever. But Asha, my sister—"

"Yes," Rakesh snapped. "I know her. I know she is your sister. I was supposed to marry her. Perhaps you remember?"

She ignored this. "Asha is very pretty. On her side, Mummy thinks no boy is good enough. For five years, we have been looking. Then you came. We were all so impressed by your picture. You are so fair. You have such a good height. You have fine shoulders. We all liked the way you part your hair on the side and the way you had grown your sideburns like a film star. You also have a very nice set of eyes. They are not quite brown.

"So Asha said yes. But then what always happens happened. Mummy started poisoning Asha's mind. She started saying she had talked to her astrologer and he said the stars were bad. That you were a widower and you would always miss your first wife. That it was very strange that your parents were so sick that they could not even meet us." (That was the excuse Rakesh had used to justify their absence.)

"Then ten days ago, Mummy almost phoned your house and said no. That was when I got very angry. We started shouting at each other. And I said, just as a thing to say, *Fine, if Asha will not marry him, then I will.*

"That was it. Then she forced me, ji. I had just said it as a thing to say only. And she forced me. She forced me to wear Asha's clothes and marry you."

"But you don't look the type to get forced."

She shrugged her shoulders. "I know what my mother thought. She thought you would expose me and bring disgrace upon the family. And then no one would ever want to marry me or Asha or Raghav. Raghav is my good brother."

"So why did you do it?"

"I was forced."

Again she began to bite her nails, but Rakesh grabbed her hand from her mouth and held her thick fingers tight. "You don't look like the type to get forced. Admit it. You wanted it also. You are making this up. You wanted it also. You secretly wished this would happen. That I wouldn't expose you. You're happy right now. You've taken revenge on your family, on your mother. Admit it—you're happy."

When Rakesh looked back days later, it was apparent he had been speaking for himself. This girl—this girl lying naked next to him—was pure revenge on his parents' expectations.

This is why he got the stupid idea into his mind that he should stay with her, that he should make love to her. She wasn't timid. She was ugly, assertive. Marrying this woman would be a true announcement of his individuality, a statement that he owed nothing to anyone, least of all his parents. He could only imagine the look on his parents' faces when they asked him tomorrow—*Is this the same girl you saw? We thought she was slimmer? What happened to her face?*

Fatness, Mummy! Fatness happened!

All his rebellions before this had been false, Rakesh realized. He did things his way but always with the subconscious goal of pleasing his parents. He had picked Asha for his second marriage himself, but she was exactly what his parents would have wanted: pretty, from the right caste, no threat to his mother in terms of sophistication. He had only hid her from them because she was so perfect.

And no one could have been more perfect than Rashmi.

His mind jetted back to his time in America. The fireside cozy of their suburban home, the two cars in the front drive ready to be ignited. Frost. How Montpelier, Vermont, smelled in the fall, like a freezing blade held up to your nose. And under the tantrum of red leaves, your feet on frostbitten gravel. How you clustered together for warmth, the big hug, the small family.

Rakesh, Rashmi, and Arjun.

He opened his eyes in shock at the image, the sensual clearness of it.

He hadn't missed America at all till now. Only during his first trip back to India, when he was fresh from the snow-suckled locales of Vermont, had he compared India to America—that, too, subconsciously. Rakesh liked to think of himself as an educated populist—*give me a wet armpit, and I'll give you a B.A.-pass nose to smell it!*—but he was also a man whose self-consciousness in America had led to an obsession with smells. Before parties, while Rashmi draped herself in Kanjeevarams, he would perfume his armpits—a blind man would have been forgiven for mistaking those pits for hairy potpourri. Once, the white particles of his solid deodorant had rained down his arms when he gesticulated wildly. "This is not dandruff!" he had explained to shocked Americans. "This is deodoruff!"

Those soapy-smelling Americans accepted him and laughed away at his lame jokes—only Rashmi would lash out at him with her tragic eyes. He would panic at those moments, forget the punchline, flail, and sink further into party-joke ignominy. He only wanted, after all, to impress his wife; he loved her so much. So, when she died, and he peered into an endless future without her, he wondered: What would he do at gatherings, at parties without Rashmi?

With whom would he go home and laugh at the foolish naïveté of these friendly Americans?

One famous question which they had spent all night laughing about, a pillow squeezed tight between them, was this: *If you don't mind my asking, I've never been to India, so forgive me, I may be thinking of the wrong animal, but, Mrs. Ahuja, is it common for people to own elephants the way people here own horses?*

And Rashmi had said to the old lady: *Why, of course, how else would I get to the airport?*

When he and Arjun were taking the plane back to India for Rashmi's cremation, that was the one line that appeared to sum up America for him.

He hated America so much. He hated it for taking Rashmi away from him, plus U.S. Air had just served him a pancake with a little packet of liquid on the side that looked *exactly* like maple syrup but was actually soy sauce, and soy sauce plus pancake was the perfect recipe for midair barf—he hated America so much that his mind exploded the one inane sentence *Do you own an elephant?* into a plan to scoff America for a lifetime. He would dedicate his life henceforth to owning an elephant in his Delhi house and riding it shamelessly through Khan Market, GK Market, South Extension, Paranthe Kee Gulley—really, whatever direction the wind blew the creature's Dumbo ears. In addition, Rakesh would dress purely in saffron, never shower, and make it a point to emit a terrific odor. He would allow his elephant to mold mountains of shit wherever it desired so that curious American tourists could follow in his wake and photograph *that Far Eastern shit*! If he was invited to a party, he would say: "Only if you invite my elephant and refuse to bring it up in conversation at any point. Because if you bring it up then it will suggest to Americans that elephants are indeed unusual in an urban Indian setting, and this will break their hearts. So what would you rather do? Maintain an icy silence—or send Americans screaming, heartbroken?" At restaurants he would throw a consumerist fit if the patron said: "Do you want a doggy bag, sir?" *Do I look like a doggy-owning sort of man to you! Are these the hands of a doggy-rider?* At night he would let the elephant rest in his driveway and scrub it like a lovesick mechanic and refer to it as PINKY. But mostly Rakesh relished the image of walking up to his parents and saying *I am dedicating myself to buying an elephant* and enjoying their stunned expressions.

Will you have some chai, they would say.

You are getting away from the point at hand.

But son, have we not been good parents? Did we not take you on the third of every full moon to the Delhi zoo from the special pass entrance?

No, you have given birth to me and led me to sadness, and now the only thing I can say to you is that I need an elephant in my life.

What about another wife?

Another wife?

They are better, no? Can be ridden too. Plus, less dung, less maintenance.

He had woken from his vision to the wailing of two-year-old Arjun—curled up in a tiny crib on the plane—and been ashamed that his vision had made no mention of Arjun and that already he was craving a new wife. He needed to remain single, wedded only to his memory of Rashmi. He had to live for the last surviving vestige of Rashmi—his son. He had to make money for Arjun's sake and not descend into depression.

But what could he do now that he had quit his PhD program?

Rakesh Ahuja crouched in the aisle seat of U.S. Airways Flight 232 and wept.

Thinking of Rashmi, Rakesh felt a flare of warmth shoot through his body. All his sexual instincts were reactivated. He wanted to make love to this strange, unattractive, gutsy girl lying next to him on the hotel bed. He made her turn away from him, held her breasts, and entered her precisely; she said nothing, though he could feel little tender jabs along the line of her spine. He thought of Rashmi the entire time they made love. Once in a while, he said a soothing word.

The end result of all this—when they lay side by side again, fully clothed, after having washed up, taking turns in the bathroom, having nothing to say—was regret. He hadn't used a condom, and this was a hideous way to make a girl lose her virginity, what did she think of him? He tried to be tender with her again, but her body reacted with stiffness. She fussily adjusted her pillow. She turned and flounced away as if they had been married for years. Rakesh wondered: Did she see him, as he saw himself now, as a monster? Or was she pleased that they were now stuck—that he couldn't possibly leave her now. What if she was pregnant? And if they were stuck, did she know what she was in for? The type of person he was?

"I think you're very pretty," he said.

Here we go.

"Thank you," she mumbled.

"Was that okay?"

"Yes."

"Did you feel good?"

He was sitting up now, arms thrown around his knees.

"Yes."

"Are you sure?"

He considered turning her over and kissing her.

"Yes."

"Good," he said.

"Good night," she said.

"Good night."

Soon she was asleep, curled away from Rakesh. He stayed awake for a few minutes, staring at the spiral striations left by the bangles on her bare arm. He kept thinking with a mixture of excitement and pity: *This is the strangest marriage of all time. We are in for a horrible life together. I will no doubt become worse with age. I've probably made her pregnant, and now I've lost all power and I will spend all my life trying to regain it. I'll blame her for everything, as I blamed my parents. And then one day, I'll no longer be a grieving widower. I'll just be an awful husband. This girl's life*, he told himself, *is finished.*

He had given himself too much credit. In the morning, when he woke, she was gone.

CHAPTER 9

BRYAN ADAMS EXPLAINS EVERYTHING (UNFORTUNATELY)

MR. AHUJA WAS SOON TO LEARN about his eldest son's band. It was past normal lunchtime and everyone was starving. He was sitting at the head of a long rectangular teak table that had been reinforced by two smaller tables at the ends. These two tables were at least six inches shorter than the main table, and so, to compensate for the makeshift extension, the taller Ahujas usually sat at the ends, carefully passing steel plates over the wooden drop. Today, however, everyone was concentrated toward Mr. Ahuja's end. Mrs. Ahuja, meanwhile, was missing, probably tending to the babies in the nursery. The children chewed boisterously. They stopped for an instant to acknowledge Arjun's presence as he glided in on his socked feet, the last to arrive. Then they gobbled. That was one feature the family shared: they were a platoon of gobblers, consuming food with a speedy, scavenging relish.

"Hello, Arjun," Mr. Ahuja said, not looking up from his plate.

"See I told you, Papa!" said Rahul. "He doesn't have a pocket on his uniform shirt."

"But it was *there once upon a time*," argued Varun from across the table.

"Address your elder brother as *Arjun bhaiya*, not *he*," said Mr. Ahuja.

"Sorry Papa," said Rahul. Then again: "But I think some goondas must have torn up his pocket. I hear this is what they are doing in stupid schools like St. Columba's. Everyone knows Modern School is the best school. Right, Varun?"

Varun and Rahul were students at Modern School (the Humayun Road branch).

"At least in Modern we don't even make pockets for our shirts, ha? So much smarter. Why make something if it is going to be torn off by bullies?" said Varun.

Rahul continued, "I wonder if he went to the principal's office and said, 'Father, please, my pocket is torn.'"

"Then Father says—'I am taking charity on you. Here is some money.'"

"And then what?"

"Then *bhaiya* must have said, 'But sir, where shall I keep this money without a pocket?'"

The two of them laughed.

But Arjun wasn't listening. He swiped a plate from the sideboard, lunged through the gap between Rita and Tanya ("Watch out, Arjun!" they shouted) and piloted the saucer from pot to pot ("Watch out, Arjun!" they shouted). The plate now heavy with food, Arjun walked, with a completely unnecessary swagger, to a spot across from his father, intensely aware of his own abrupt theatricality. He sat down. He shoveled food in an unbroken rhythm. He didn't speak to anyone; no one spoke to him. He wanted to continue the silence until someone noticed the sullen beauty of his motions and initiated conversation, he wanted the crowd of children to see how things were done in real life, with silence and purpose and syncopation, that real men didn't even consider the crowds swelling around them, they knew women were drawn to haughty sexy silences, that . . .

He leaned across the table and shouted: "Papa, I am in a rock band."

Mr. Ahuja said, "Really? Great, if you're comfortable in it."

"Thanks, Papa," said Arjun. He was unable to contain his incredulity. "Thanks a lot for your kind words."

He speared his spoon through a mound of rice and rose from the table in a huff.

Watching Arjun leave, Mr. Ahuja felt defeated. What had he said now? The commingling of the other children's voices was not unlike that of a dying herd of cattle. His tough day found apt regurgitation in the shapeless and tasteless food his wife always served up—and she didn't even cook! All she had to do was order the servants! The vegetable sellers came right up to their doorstep! Everyone wanted to sell to the Ahuja army! Yet the food—aalu-ghobi, tinda, daal—was a runny yellow mishmash, a marshland of masalas, it offered no visual solace to beaten taste buds. His kids seemed to enjoy it all the same—poor bastards. They didn't know better, how could they? His wife was the highest index of quality they'd experienced. He'd left them in her clutches. He was an absent busybody father, a gene transmitter, a blur of power in their lives. He hadn't even informed them that he'd resigned—such news took a huge toll on them, poor things, they had short memories, they cried angrily on their father's behalf, badmouthed his political rivals, once Varun was hospitalized with a scalding fever.

Thanks to the food, Mr. Ahuja felt a little ill himself; he regretted sending the peremptory message to the SPM—his boss!—the one person who'd done so much for his political career. Still, what was done was done. He was here to talk to Arjun. He splashed his spoon into the yogurt bowl and decided to follow the boy to the nursery through the cramped house.

Arjun was standing before Mrs. Ahuja with one arm furiously rocking Gita's crib.

Mrs. Ahuja, of course, was knitting.

"Mama," said Arjun. "I can't help you with the feeding today. I have to go practice with my band."

Arjun knew Mr. Ahuja was listening, and so he delivered the statement as forcefully and dramatically as he could.

"Pass me the wool," she said. "This sweater is to be made with two colors."

Arjun had a vivid flash of his childhood: a prison with bars made of wool, huge knitted cobwebs blooming around the house. At night, the two rooms—each of which held five children—looked like a sighing coral reef, veins of yarn wrapped around each child. Their mother perpetually in the thrall of morning sickness, moving from pregnancy to pregnancy with such haste that there was almost no spot in the house where she *hadn't* given birth. Luckily, Arjun only had to share a room with ten-year-old Rishi and twelve-year-old Varun.

"Mama! I cannot stay home today to feed the children," Arjun shouted.

"Are you listening to your son?" Mrs. Ahuja said. "No sense of family he is having. One day in the week he is to help and even that he cannot do."

Mr. Ahuja turned to Mrs. Ahuja. "Sangita! He is upset because you are making him wear short pants. Look how he is growing! Maybe you should knit for your elder children, have you ever considered this? He doesn't have a pocket on his shirt. And he is wearing short pants. The other boys must be mocking him at school. Correct?"

"What?" they both asked.

"Are you not in short pants?" Mr. Ahuja asked.

"Papa, I am in a *rock band. A rock band*."

"See, what animalistic way he is talking in already," Mrs.

Ahuja said, casting off a stitch. "Soon he will have long hair and be chanting in Rishikesh with some babus."

How did Mama know about the Beatles? This blew Arjun's mind.

Mr. Ahuja was less impressed. "Arre! The boy is wanting to do something, so let him?"

"Pass me the wool, Arjun," she said.

Arjun was upset and did as he was told. But the way he handed his mother the ball of yarn—letting it drop into her lap, unspooling in the air—was his way of saying: *Why can't you argue more with me? Why can't you beg me to stay? Why can't you say to him—I can't bring up so many children alone, I need Arjun?* After all, in the past, he had been on duty *daily*. He had been the head constable who kept the peace. He loomed over the children while Sangita fell asleep under the smooth spell of the massage-wali; learned to hip-hold a child the right way before he learned to grip a cricket bat; never wore a shirt that wasn't acid-washed by yellow drool; always agreed to sprawl out on the carpet and roll dinky cars along a distracted baby's line of vision; taught each of the children to suck their respective thumbs (he'd demonstrate for hours on end, glug-glug-glug, claiming thumbs tasted like chocolate) in order to allow for a little silence in the house; instilled a fear of ghosts to keep them glued to their beds at night; covered up for Sangita when she set fire to one of the (baby-free) cribs with a candle she was carrying to her makeshift shrine; and even made polite conversation with her about her favorite TV shows.

Then, inexplicably, a year ago, he'd been relieved of his post, forced into retirement, replaced by Varun and Rita, and now he missed being in charge. If his Mama wanted him on duty only once a week, she couldn't have him at all.

Arjun stormed out of the house, the screen door crackling behind him. His parents didn't even care that he had a secret life. They could never be shocked out of their complacency. He could have become the most famous rock star in the world, he could have had three #1 hits, a Grammy-nominated album that the critics called the "enraged embodiment of Indian teenage life at the outset of the millennium"—he might even have flared through the countryside on a grand tour (at this moment, he paused and imagined himself on a stage with a mountain of amplifiers stacked sky-high behind him, the stage a shiny gray soon to be dulled by a rainstorm of pink panties, the microphone shivering with all the delicacy of a phallus caught in fellatio and the giant sea of heads floating beneath him like hairy algae, among them only one face visible, one beaming almond-shaped face)—Aarti's face. He was the most famous rock star in the world and Aarti knew it. He imagined Aarti standing in the front row at a concert, both of them staring sweetly at each other.

Keeping the vision before him at all times (he saw her like the afterimage of a light bulb, in purple), he took an auto to Ravi's place and clutched the guardrail tight. Minutes after he arrived, Anurag and Deepak breezed into the driveway in a Santro, guitars strapped on their backs at diametrically opposite angles so as to produce the effect of bad-ass symmetry. They walked into Ravi's tiny room for a conference.

"You won't believe what happened today, yaar," said Ravi.

"What, yaar?"

He narrated an unlikely story involving an ice cream seller, a traffic light, and a hot babe.

"Then?"

"She totally winked at me."

"Cool. Can we start with 'Summer of '69'?" Arjun asked.

"Bryan Adams?" said Deepak. "You're being a metrosexual now?"

"We are only playing Metallica style tunes here," echoed Anurag.

"But I am the lead singer!" said Arjun. "I provide the emotion. I cannot provide emotion from a song by people who eat—who eat rust for fun."

"Oh, that's a good line for a song. Or title. *Eat Rust for Fun*," said Ravi, defending Arjun.

"Exactly!" said Anurag. "For a Metallica song!"

They settled on Bon Jovi as an acceptable compromise.

At first that day, the tunes of the band were only fleeting bouts of melody, wisps of song that arose from the (clearly random) intersection of instruments. The beat seemed to throb beneath the guitars, but then when the guitars went awry the beat was all you heard, the song became nothing but Arjun screaming past the pounding of percussion and you had to start all over again and you'd stop singing and the guitars would stop going, and only the stupid drummer, stupid self-hating Ravi, would keep thrashing away. It was as if he had decided already, obviously, that *he* was the center of the band or, if not the center, then at least the backbone and you know, time and tide and Ravi's drums waited for none, so you'd just have to kind of sit there till the boy had had his share of showing off. It was his house. They couldn't say anything.

Instead, they sweated the same sweat and ran afoul of each other; blamed each other for not using enough Ax Spray; at one point Ravi walked in from the bathroom and misted his bedroom with deodorant, leaving a damp residue on the walls which dilated and contracted with the same ominous intensity as monsoon seepage. As for the boys, their eyes stung as they leaned into the PC and tried to swipe tabs and chords off the Internet. What was band-width but the breadth of experience a band could copy-paste off the Internet? What was evolution but homing in on the easiest songs? Clapton was out; so were The Eagles; so was Metallica. Bands like Staind and Oasis and Bryan Adams and Steppenwolf were stripped down to a mere progression of power chords, their song-length magic fissioned into tiny fragments that Deepak bombarded over and over with his Stratocaster, his feet clocking out a number of effects from the amp. In particular, he focused on the whoosh of the UNDER-WATER pedal.

Like any real band at its first practice session, about three-fourths of the time was spent fussily tuning the guitars and screwing in the loose plates of the drum kit. This gave Arjun plenty of time to study the lyrics. He logged onto the Internet for inspiration. He wanted to track down every last bit of Bryan Adams trivia that Google.com could muster. Wrists tensed in parallel, he was disturbed to find that every American site mocked him—firstly, and Arjun thought, rather unfairly, for being Canadian, and secondly, for being "schmaltzy." A sonata of solidarity sparked into the keyboard from Arjun's hands. He searched selectively for fan sites. He looked up the meaning of *schmaltzy*. It didn't exist on WordLocator. (He had misspelled it.) He lost respect for the slangy denigrators. Still the evidence kept accumulating. Bryan Adams figured at #49 in a list of "100 Most Common Reasons Couples Break Up." There was a site started by a Swede who'd been rescued from the verge of suicide by Bryan's life-affirming hits album *So Far So Good* ("It cuts like a knife/ oh yeah / but it feels so right" being the operative lines here) but had now, with the accrued knowledge of "so many years, tears, and fears," realized that perhaps it was better to *commit suicide* than be a Bryan Adams fan. "Certainly, one receives more respect when one undertakes the former rather than the latter," the final line of the opening page stated.

Distasteful parody, Arjun thought. He posted a few angry comments on the site's message board.

> 1stly I don't belive yr Swedish. Swedes are respectable people, committing suicide with or w/o music. You are American. 2ndly, why commit suicide? Pls give your address/phone and I will

gladly use the reel of my destroyed tape of 18 Til I Die to fish out your intestines via your mouth, okay? Death guaranteed, promise.

Further, before you commit suicide to end your "hard knock life" here is a picture of me.

He posted the picture of a malnourished African child. Then another message.

Sorry for previous, just joking!!!!!Picture however is okay.
PS>>>Have you ever really loved a woman?

He posted a picture of the actress Aishwarya Rai.

But he hadn't even gotten to the reviews.

Bryan Adams's hit song "Everything I Do" occupied the #1 position on the UK Charts for a record sixteen weeks. The song itself is best described as a ballad-to-permanently-put-an-end-to-the-genre-of-ballads. With his constipated I-ate-Rod-Stewart-for-breakfast vocals, a steadfast desire to rhyme desire with fire, night with right (as in, I am going to do [something sleazy] with you tonight / how could something wrong / feel so right, a construct he has used twenty-one times in his career), liar with desire, fire with higher (ire, mire, choir, dire, sire are all considered too verbose for his oeuvre) and truly massive ability to insinuate his god-awful crap into just about any soundtrack, Bryan Adams is STILL the best singer-songwriter to emerge from Canada in years.

Racists! Hating Canadians!
A Customer Comment on Amazon said:

The real problem is that Bryan Adams lacks edge. He is too syrupy to even be a guilty pleasure.

Now this simply killed him. Guilty pleasure? Excuse me? Clearly, people in the West were so overdosed on luxuries that they'd begun to crave art that was damaging, challenging, difficult, edgy. Perhaps they should come to India for a day. Take a walk in a slum. Get hit by a scooter and lose a couple of limbs while the gathered crowd officiated over your wallet. Feed some suicidal farmers. Or wait: Wasn't it better for a farmer to commit suicide anyway than to be rich and listen to Bryan Adams? Yes, of course. Stupid fools. They'd start appreciating their so-called "guilty pleasures" if they'd lived through tragedy.

But despite his mental tirade, Arjun was shaken. He'd come into this thinking that Bryan Adams was his last remaining friend and had learned, much to his consternation, that *he* was Bryan Adams's only friend as well.

Then Bryan Adams betrayed him. It happened in the body of an interview that was posted online.

> INTERVIEWER: As long as we are on the subject of "Summer of '69," just how autobiographical is the song?
>
> ADAMS: Some parts are autobiographical, but the title comes from the idea of 69 as a metaphor for sex. Most people thought it was about the year 1969.

"Did you see this?" asked Arjun. "Did you fucking goddamn see this?"

Ravi wasn't interested. "We should be practicing man—you should be practicing."

"Sorry man."

"No, no, it's fine man," said Ravi, "but we need to decide what ten songs we'll start with. Then I need to make sure I'm timed correct with Deepak. We also need balance, man. Balance. How many acoustic songs, how many ballads, how much smashing? You know? Also, are we doing covers or originals?"

No one listened to Ravi. He started to bitch. He emphasized casually that his bandmates were fags and tapped his drums with a light feminine touch to show that he wasn't exactly thrilled that they were practicing in his house.

Arjun conceded, "Let's do this, Ravs. You can pick the songs, okay? Any songs you like."

Big mistake.

Soon they were playing "The End" by The Doors, an eight-minute odyssey during which the band members made various, disarming discoveries about one another, as men often do during long trips. Most monumental of which was that Anurag didn't really know how to play the bass guitar. This had passed unnoticed at first because Anurag had obviously spent plenty of time studying the *angle* at which a guitar must be slung over one's shoulder so as to appear unfailingly cool, and also knew that C-Major and D never sounded bad. In fact, if it wasn't for Deepak, who derived his confidence from deriding others, they might never have noticed.

But now even Arjun came down on Anurag. "Anu, you're a bloody bastard."

They remanded him, in a historic decision, to the spot of synthesizer player—a decision that saddened Ravi but one, as he would acknowledge months later, that added a dimension to their sound that none of their compatriots, especially those fuckers Orange Street and Parikrama, could lay claim to.

So it came to be. Of the four of them—Ravi, who asked poignantly why Indians didn't have garages; Deepak, generally using his sporty sadism to deride his bandmates; and Anurag, who was no longer pretend-plucking his guitar—only Arjun continued having fun. He was screaming. He was singing into a pencil box. He was opening and closing the pencil box, taunting his own lips. He went to the bathroom while a long solo occurred. He rapped a snippet from 2Pac when it seemed apt ("All Eyez on Me"). Launched into esoteric mumbo-jumbo ("Calling on Onion Transit, Calling on Onion Transit, Radio Delete Europe") while craving a glass of lemon juice. One minute he'd be serenading; the next he was reminiscent of a Doberman tied to a gate barking at oncoming traffic.

The question is: How is he singing?

"How am I singing?" Arjun sneered.

"Okay. Good. Fine," said Ravi. "But try not to scream. Actually: Don't. My Dada and Dadi are sleeping two rooms from here. You're screaming nonstop. Anyway, control it; otherwise your voice will go. There is no good way to fix that. You can drink water and hot chocolate, but—"

"But screaming is what all these fellows do."

"That's true. But—"

Troubled silence.

"Let's suicide him," said Deepak.

Seconds later, they piled on Arjun, and this time his screams were real. The band had attained its homoerotic ideal.

When they started their next song—once they had tuned and tuned and tuned—the electricity went. At this time the four boys did not recognize how big and important a role power-cuts-as-sound-effect would play in the historic sound they were inching toward; how the Delhi Vidyut Power Board collapsing was the sound of a million people moaning in one syncopation, one forced fadeout of a guitar, only Arjun's voice and the drums floating over the remains of what had once been a song.

But the unplugged guitarists improvised. Somehow Anurag and Deepak were able to match the twanging of their bass and rhythm, and now Arjun started to croak and he closed his eyes and the chords clicked into place—and he couldn't do it. He couldn't bring himself to imagine Aarti and the song at once. When he sang, he lost Aarti. The small, quiet, dark room made him self-conscious, as if he were singing into a wall of judging listeners. As if he were in a tomb, in a womb, trying to scream his way out.

"I can't sing in such a small space," he admitted, speaking into the wall. He licked the wallpaper sensually.

The band members approved of his histrionics.

"Man, that's good," said Ravi. "Like whatshisname—Jim Morrison? Kiss?"

"You can even wear mascara."

"No, I really can't sing," Arjun insisted.

Mrs. Mehta—Ravi's mother—tended to agree. "What are you children doing?" she asked, stepping into the room. "All the neighbors are calling me and asking things? Please do not be doing this. Here are five hundred rupees, go to the market and do your no-good lazy thuggery over there."

And they did, though not without an air of dejection. Their first practice had failed. They ate ice cream and ogled girls in GK Market. Arjun felt a little relieved that no one had pinned the band's failure on his complete inability to sing. As they walked through the market, he expressed his deep desire to scream and the impossibility of viscerally exercising his talent in the company of such mean neighbors. He extolled the virtues of dressing in a tight white T-shirt and jeans (which he would procure for all them, of course). He spoke at length about his vision for the band, an intersection of traditional Indian values (conveyed lyrically) with a distinctly American tradition associated with Bryan Adams (conveyed through tight jeans).

"But he's a fucking Canadian, you fool," said Ravi.

Arjun looked at Ravi and replied solemnly: "We need a better place to practice."

They were sitting in Barista, sipping cold coffees animated with whirling clouds of sugar. Somehow they had lost track of the hours, whiling them away playing video games in United Arcade and putting their feet up on tables at all the new coffee shops that had opened up in GK.

Ravi said, "How about your house? You have a big garden. Your electricity never goes. Your dad gives speeches there—so there must be amps. We can also go on your roof. If there's noise we'll go acoustic."

All this was true, but Arjun wanted to say: the problems are numerous too. To begin with, he had always maintained that he had only six siblings, not twelve. Using a special route through the house—one that took him past the kitchen, with its constant screech of mixies and pressure cookers, and wound around the nursery—he could prevent his friends from noticing at least five of his brothers and sisters who'd be bangled around the TV in Mama's room, playing on the old, outdated Mega-Drive video console. But then: the cluster of toothbrushes in the bathroom. The elongated 12 x 30 family photos on the wall. The fifteen table-mats on the table. The shoe rack that was more shoe than rack. The skyscrapers of folded laundry on the peninsular outcropping of the ironing board. The guest bedroom stuffed with pyramids of toilet paper and ointments and tampons and plastic-wrapped diapers and old-fashioned airtight jars containing Lifebuoy Soap, flaxseeds, roasted garlic cloves, gond gum, mango preserves, *Parle G* biscuits—a history of Mama's cravings. It wasn't worth the risk. He hadn't invited his friends to his house in *years*.

And then there was Shankar, that nosy, boisterous servant who existed in an oscillating state of being-fired and quitting, of being drunk and sober, of being playful and interfering, so on, so forth, *ad infinitum*. The last time he was fired, he had written a letter to Mrs. Ahuja—that torturer of servants—saying that he hoped he was reborn as a dog in the Ahuja household, because a dog, he suspected, would be treated better than a servant (he was right). Luckily, Mr. Ahuja got his hands on this letter as well, took pity on the poor man whose handwriting was smudged from the very-same rains that had destroyed his house in Ranikhet (so he claimed), leaving him with nothing, only the cell phone he had once purchased in installments, which in any case was no good in the Himalayas, where he had tried calling from (he claimed) before writing this letter about the prospects of *life as a dog in the Ahuja household*. The point was, Shankar had a strange hold on everyone. He was a season, returning always, fiercer than before, globally warmed by the TV in the kitchen. He had an opinion on everything. He insisted on humming, for instance, the Offspring song "Pretty Fly for a White Guy," which he had heard Arjun play on repeat. This awful cooption—this humming by a man who had no idea what the song was about (nor did Arjun, he thought it was about a prettily designed zipper on a pant)—was acceptable only because no one else knew the song.

Arjun himself was humming the song. He nodded vaguely at Ravi and wondered what everyone was doing at home. It was already five in the evening. Arjun was almost never away from the house this long without permission (even though he was sixteen! Sixteen!); he burned with pride as he imagined his parents' anxiety, their desperate calls to his friends' homes.

Or maybe, he realized, they wouldn't notice he was missing. It was perfectly plausible in a house with thirteen children.

"So?" said Ravi. "Your house?"

"I'll ask my Dad," said Arjun.

CHAPTER 10

MR. AHUJA RIGS THE POLLS

MR. AHUJA HAD NOT IGNORED Arjun's rock band. He couldn't ignore it. He had followed Arjun to the threshold of the nursery and lost him for the second time in one day. He reached down and lifted up baby Vikram from his crib, held him to his shoulder, burps and all, and was aware suddenly of the immense distance—the strained ropes of time and space—that separated him from his youngest child, the sheer number of intervening boys and girls whom he'd birthed to undertake—in effect—the bidding of the father, their years of training at child rearing slowly cutting away the cumulative minutes Rakesh spent changing Vikram's diapers and coochy-cooing on his knees beside the crib. The issues at the top—Arjun, for example—could keep one busy forever. To plunge through the system was to feel, at times, like one's intelligence was being wasted, that a command once given or a lesson once taught would automatically transmit itself in gathering concentration, like DDT in the human body or wealth in an economy or each-one-in-a-teach-one, to the underprivileged voiceless baby. What was a baby but a multi-limbed package of stimuli? What was a baby compared to Rita's first period or Varun's attempt to set fire to the front garden or Sahil's discovery that the Coke was so adulterated it tasted of ink? What was he doing kissing his baby when he ought to be talking to Arjun?

The thought—its strains of cost-benefit analysis—made him feel disgusted.

"I'm going to tell Arjun about his mother today," he said, not turning around to face Mrs. Ahuja, "when he comes back."

"Good," she said.

Mr. Ahuja said, "Good? *Good?* You don't believe me or what?"

"I do," said Mrs. Ahuja. "I believe."

But Mr. Ahuja knew she didn't. He had used the threat of telling Arjun the secret some one hundred forty-five times in their marriage.

"Then?" Mr. Ahuja said.

"Haan-ji?"

"That's all?"

"Yes."

"Goddamn it Sangita, it is hundred percent *useless* talking to you."

In the drawing room, Mr. Ahuja's children greeted him with greater enthusiasm: they told Mr. Ahuja that Arjun was in a rock band to impress a girl.

"So who is this girl?" asked Mr. Ahuja.

"She goes on his bus I think," volunteered Aneesha. She was eight and still sucked her thumb. She claimed it tasted like tutti-frutti.

"She owes *what*?" asked Mr. Ahuja. He undid the strap of his slippers. The house at this hour looked particularly tasteless and shabby—the tables and chairs painted a rudimentary white, the paintings on the wall cocked to the side, a muddy pair of footprints slowly turning the color of dusk, the gloss of dust on the cabinets giving everything an aura of mindless preservation.

The sofa—covered with plastic—crackled loudly as Mr. Ahuja pushed himself up to his full height. The children bent to touch his feet, then withdrew as they encountered the force field of odor protecting them, and said, "She goes on Arjun's bus."

"She knows about us? And she still wants to come into this household? This mad place? Look at all of you. How am I going to get you children married? Eh? Can you imagine us living as *a joint family*?" Mr. Ahuja slapped his thigh.

The children guffawed.

"Do you want to have ice cream?" said Mr. Ahuja. "Come. Let's go to Khan Market."

It was four in the afternoon, and they crossed the street to Khan Market with thrilling success. The two guards came out of their conical hut, blocked the road with giant yellow barriers and provided the children with safe passage (much to the dismay of the honking cars) all the way to Barista. Barista was the Ahuja family's coffee chain of choice. The old dusty bookshops and fancy foreign-goods-stocked stores were squashed between tiny cement pillars; most of the shutters were drooping. Small galaxies of dust swirled on the pavement. Enormous white shop signs with red lettering were spread the length of the market like rotten teeth about to chomp into the ground.

The server at Barista asked if this was a birthday party. They had a special cake.

Mr. Ahuja said no.

A school trip?

"No," said Mr. Ahuja. "Get eight cold coffees. And pull together four tables."

He didn't foresee the terrible havoc caffeine and sugar would wreak on his already restless children. Instead, he sat them down around the tables—Sahil and Aneesha on his lap—and said, "Now. I want to tell you something about Arjun. You remember I was married once before I married your Mama, correct?"

He saw the bewilderment furrow across their faces; they looked like old, exaggerated Ahujas. Incidents of nose-picking suddenly multiplied. Straws found themselves sucking at empty glasses; they grumbled rudely with air. The children looked at one another and scratched away at their ears.

Then they said, "Correct."

"Correct."

"Yes, Papa."

"Yes."

"Yes."

Only Sahil and Aneesha and Rishi were silent, scraping dirt from their uncut nails. Mr. Ahuja indicated them with the back of his palm. "You little ones probably don't remember."

Mr. Ahuja at it again! Divide and rule!

Sahil and Aneesha and Rishi protested. "Of course yes Papa!"

"What are you *saying*?" Tanya sneered. "You were too little."

"Yes, beta, Tanya is right. It was a long time ago. Before any of you were born, in fact. Before I married your mama even. When I was younger, I was married to another lady. As you know. But she, God bless her, passed away in a car accident. You remember me telling you, correct?" he asked gruffly. "Real tragedy it was. Like the movies. Unforgettable."

"Un for get bal," said Rahul.

"Of course, yes."

"Hundred percent."

"Yes Papa."

"Very sad."

"Chhoo chhad."

"It was a Contessa, right, Papa?"

"A WHAT?" Mr. Ahuja said.

"A Contessa Car."

"Uh, yes—Contessa. Anyway. As you know, *she* was the one who was Arjun's real mother. You know this right? Why are you all looking so surprised?"

Surprise was not the word, no—they looked like they'd all just been held down forcefully and given ten injections to their buttocks.

The Insect-O-Flash device at the counter crackled as more and more flies electrocuted themselves on the four parallel bright tube lights.

"Not surprised, Papa," they lied.

"Yes Papa. We know about Arjun."

"That's why he doesn't like when hero in movies says to villain, *Have you drunk your mother's milk?* He feels like a villain when he is with Mama."

"Ughzactly."

Mr. Ahuja felt bad that he was playing them—but what choice did he have? Better for them to suppress their surprise and mimic adulthood. Better for them to trick themselves into familiarity with the shocking news—to waste their energies combing their memories rather than aggressively posing questions.

"Yes. Good. Very good memory," said Mr. Ahuja. "All those years of feeding you duffers cod-liver oil has worked, eh? But yes. We never talk about it because Arjun was only three when your mama became *his* mama. Do you remember anything from when you were three? No, naah? So that is what I wanted to say. Arjun was feeling a little upset because he's the only one of you who isn't born from Mama and he doesn't even remember his real Mama. He feels left out. He thinks Mama and you all act differently toward him."

Now the children were caught. Having nodded their way through this manipulative speech, they could not issue a denial. Couldn't say they had no idea what their Papa was talking about. Instead, they tried to act cool. Tried to pretend they remembered and had, in fact, mistreated Arjun. Breathed heavily through their mouths.

"So basically he's a stepson, naah," said Tanya, translating for the other children. At twelve, she considered herself to be their representative. She was buying time.

"Stepson, yes," said Varun. "Ughzactly." He was secretly wondering how much Arjun would have to pay him to keep the secret.

"This tho I knew," Rahul lied. He itched to put the news on his blog.

"Henh?" said Mr. Ahuja. "What is this you're saying? No beta. Arjun's not a stepson! He's my son. He has my blood. If a mosquito bit me and then bit you and bit Arjun, it would be as confused as a person who drinks Diet Pepsi and Diet Coke one after the other. He is my son only. He is as much my son as any of you—"

"But I'm a girl," said Rita.

"Yes, yes, beta. As much my son as you are my daughter.

He just came from a different mother. So he's *my* real son and your Mama's stepson. That is all you need to know."

"So he *is* a stepson," Tanya said, nodding her head gravely at the crowd.

"Like in Cinderella?" said Varun excitedly.

"No stupid," Rita shushed. "That was a *stepdaughter*."

"None of this *step* nonsense," said Mr. Ahuja. "Technically he is a half-brother."

"What's technically?" asked Sahil.

"Through a *special treaty*," said Rita. "*Technically* Britain ruled India. That kind of thing."

"No, stupid," said Tanya. "It means *by law*."

"And what is a treaty exactly, Tanya? Tell me?"

"You are the true stepdaughter!" Tanya hissed. "You witch!"

"Who is a stepdaughter?" asked Mr. Ahuja.

"Haan-ji?"

"Who is a stepdaughter?" Mr. Ahuja repeated. "Please speak up!"

"No Papa," said Tanya, "what I was saying was—what I was saying was that *Mama* treats Arjun bhaiya like a step*daughter*. That was why I said stepdaughter. She says to us: Don't let him pick up the babies. Don't let him change diapers. He can't play with your toys. Tell him to do homework instead."

"Really?" said Mr. Ahuja, feigning surprise. His own commands were being blamed on Sangita, but he had no intention of clarifying this. "Well, then, you all have to stand up for your bhaiya. You have to tell Mama that bhaiya is the same as all of you. Say to her—if bhaiya is step, then we are also step!"

"And if any of *you* ever treat him like step or ever say anything—" He comically pointed to his clenched fist.

"But Papa. We wouldn't do that. He's our bhaiya!"

"Yes, we love bhaiya."

"He's our favorite bhaiya."

"Yes. He wipes me very hard."

Wipes me very hard?

"He teaches me maths."

Mr. Ahuja looked around at his children. They were so eager to please; their small brown limbs were restless; cheap plastic digital watches slid up and down their wrists; major kicking battles were underway beneath the table. He crinkled his eyebrows and said, "But what if I died and your Mama said you should be mean to him? Then? Then what would you do? You'd forget everything I said?"

It was a trick question. They answered accordingly.

"Papa you will never die," said Sahil. A tear rolled down his cheek.

Then everyone started crying. Soft silent tears. Fake tears.

"Papa don't die. We love you more."

"Yes Papa. We listen to you, not Mama."

"I love you Papa."

"I love you Papa."

"I love you more than Mama."

Mr. Ahuja hugged them one by one, accepting the compliments gracefully. "No, no bacha. Don't be like this. I was only saying. I will live for many many years. I'll make sure Mama is not mean."

It was such an easy victory—he was an emotional blackmailer, they were drama queens—and yet he felt ecstatic. That was all he wanted from life: A vote of confidence. Proof that even at the rate of an hour a day he could outperform Sangita in popularity, that no matter what he did in his political life, they'd love him. They were the reason he stayed in politics—they sanctified his corruption and confirmed his charisma. Even his youngest children, those who hadn't learned the deceptions of language, who couldn't speak at all and hence couldn't fall for his gregarious sentences, trusted him utterly and completely. He was shaped to be trusted (his head hunched forward kindly). He was an upturned trumpet of honesty (his hands were always thrown up in glee). He had such brutish powers of telepathy (he misheard the way one should). His incisors sank so wonderfully into meat (he taught them to love tandoori chicken). He could tell they loved him when he held them up with a mythical straightening of the elbows; when they gnawed at his knees; when they confided in him; when they replied to the long e-mails he sent them from the road, each one jittery and show-offy with Mr. Ahuja's memory for details.

Yes, thought Mr. Ahuja: If they resented Arjun for his closeness with their Papa, they also probably valued him for it. Mr. Ahuja relaxed. All he had to do now was talk to Arjun. "One final thing," he said. "You all have to promise you will not *ever*—I am saying *ever*—tell Arjun anything I have said today. You will *never* call him a stepbrother or a half-brother or anything. You will behave just like you all have been acting, okay? Understood? Otherwise I'll send you all to a hostel. If even one of you tells Arjun anything I will send all of you to a hostel, understand? I'm serious. I'm very, very serious."

CHAPTER II

THE BITTER HALF

A HEADSTART MEANS NOTHING if you have no wish to escape, and Sangita—*Mrs. Ahuja*, heavens—hadn't wished to escape. She was twenty-six and too bewildered by her sudden initiation into sex the night before to go much further than the hotel gate. There she stood in bright sunlight and tossed her gold veil and swirled her monstrous dupatta to ventilate her fevered skin. Growing up, Sangita had thought herself so hideous that she was certain she'd never touch a man in her life, let alone sleep with him, and so sex for her had become a clinical obsession, a phenomenon to be chased in booklets and movies and gossip, her physical awareness of the act as flimsy as the wings of a butterfly you catch between your fingers for a second before it sputters away. On her wedding night, she'd felt as if she were hovering above herself, wafting, praying. Her mother had told her nothing about the formalities of intercourse. She didn't bring any sexual dowry into the marriage. She complied readily when Rakesh said *Let's at least have sex*, because, well, *Why not?*

How else would she know?

The pleasure had been momentary—an island marooned in a night of awfulness—but pleasure it was. She awoke to a drooling man and urgent practicalities. She was married *and* sexed *and* disgraced, and a heap of trouble lay in store for her unless she alerted her family, frazzled them onto a train with their terrific rolls of bedding thumping behind them, and disappeared into the mist-guzzling elevations of Dalhousie forever. There, she'd give birth to Rakesh's child—which she was no doubt carrying (Sangita's rampant superstitions about sex and pregnancy were to be outdone only by her fertility)—and here was the tragedy: Rakesh would never know about it. Her mother, the famous Mummy, would never allow the child to reunite with its father. Instead it'd be reared by the entire sad-sack group of Mummy Papa Sangita Asha Raghav. A family together forever, the fruition of her Mummy's plan.

Everything she'd told Rakesh the previous night about her family had been true.

Unfortunately, as soon as Sangita was cast out into the vista-flattening heat of the hotel parking lot, she realized: Delhi was a foreign city. There was nowhere to go. She'd told him the truth, and now she was at his mercy.

Also, she wanted to have sex again.

So she waited around, rehearsing a look of desperation on the drivers mopping their fancy cars. They responded with puzzled looks—as did Rakesh, who had jogged up behind her in a blast of sandy wind.

"What are you doing?" he said.

He was panting. She was standing. She admitted as much. "I am standing only. I did not want to bother you in morning-time—"

"Okay, okay." He looked slightly irritated but was quick to swat it away with a gaze of fierce earnestness. "Look," he said, "I'm sorry about last night. I hope you don't think I am that sort of person. I was very surprised obviously. But I think we should stay married. This may sound strange, but I liked what you said. I liked that you were honest with me. You were very brave."

There was nothing to say to this. She could not understand it. His stubble was dark and velvety and sweaty on the cheeks, and sparse around his mouth. It was as if he'd been beaten up and then bandaged in black gauze.

"I think we should stay married," he repeated. "I believe in fate."

Fate! Ha! Sangita could have died laughing.

Her fate, after all, was to be exposed. Not knowing what else to do, she went with him to his parents' house.

The parents said, "It's very nice to meet you Asha."

"You also, naah, Mama, you are so confused," clucked Rakesh. "Her name's not Asha. It's—" He didn't know her name. Unbelievable.

"Sangita, ji," said Sangita. "Asha was my pet-name."

They were aghast, the poor parents. They kept apologizing. They looked so embarrassed they were about to die.

"They are very nice," Sangita said, when they got in the car. "Such sweet people they are."

She wondered: *Was I good in bed? Is he taking me home? Is this really Arjun sitting in my lap? Is it possible Rakesh finds me attractive?*

Rakesh shook his head. "Nice, my foot. You know what they are probably saying right now? I don't know where Rakesh picked this maid. She can't even speak good English."

He seemed to take immense pleasure in the description.

The trouble from the start was sex. She wanted to have sex and she wanted the world to know she was having sex. Denied. Rakesh never touched her again till she was significantly pregnant. He cooed at Arjun and collapsed at night, tired, heatstruck from rallies. His feet and arms twitched while he slept, as if to shake off any contact with Sangita. Sangita quickly exhausted all her techniques: tying her dupatta so it angled deftly past a nipple, wearing a flimsy blouse with the top button broken, co-cuddling Arjun with Rakesh.

This last "technique" irritated Rakesh the most, and one night, when he returned from a campaign in Himachal, he turned to Sangita and said, "Put him down."

Sangita had been holding Arjun up by the armpits to Rakesh and saying, "Say hello to your Papa. Hello, Papa."

Rakesh repeated, "Put him down. Can't you see he wants

to be put down? This is not a humorous matter. I am going to lose the election. I've been wasting my time. You have also been wasting your time. He is not your son. He is not going to be your son. When he can say more words, I'm going to tell him about his mother and then he won't care for you or thank you for these things you are doing, understand?"

But she didn't want to be thanked. She had immense affection for the child. She'd spent all day cooking kheer for Arjun and singing him songs and shampooing his gorgeous curly hair, and she'd gladly have done this even without the promise of sex.

I understand your hurt, she wanted to say. *But please don't do this to me. Please understand. I love your son like my own.* But how could she? Instead, Sangita watched Rakesh lie bareback on the marble floor, his head spasming against the cold hard surface. Later that night, he slid under the bed and wept, and even from above, half-awake, she could feel the soft thunder of his throat as he tried to control another outburst of tears. His hand poked out from the shadows like a baby's fist, unreasonably tight. Every so often, his head would hit the boards and there would be silence, as if he had died for a few minutes, acknowledged his own ostrichlike comedy, and gone silent with self-consciousness. And Sangita, who was humped down on the bed with grief, would think then: *Why will you not let me see you? Why, why, why?*

God granted her this wish to see in the most spiteful way: Rakesh won the election. He became obsessed with himself.

Now he couldn't stop boasting about his success. "I'd never thought a man of my background could be in politics. Funny thing it is, eh? Most of these people are not even Class-10-pass. Did you pass Class-10? Good, good. Sometimes I feel bad that my Hindi is not good. But then I just start saying how America is terrible, and the buggers all listen—because I've lived in America! Because I am an outsider they are all more trusting!"

Sangita proudly and dutifully broadcast this information to the two friends she had made in the neighborhood.

What she couldn't handle or broadcast, however, was Rakesh's reverence for Rupa Bhalla, the head of the SZP Party. She was his mentor. He was positively lovelorn. "Rupa Bhalla—what an amazing woman she is. Her husband died and one month later she is taking the party to victory. Really. You heard, nah? He was run over by an advanced harvester. What a brilliant lady, I tell you. She is like a second mother to me. You can talk to her about anything. She is so self-aware also. She told me: 'Rakesh, I am sorry you also have to drink the rosewater I dip my feet in, I feel as if I am the leader of a religious cult.' And I said: 'Madam, that is exactly what you should appear like!'"

This last line elicited verbal revenge from Mrs. Ahuja. She said, "I don't know what is happening—the potty Arjun is making these days is shaped like those cheap bananas which are green. Can you explain, ji?"

If he could talk about his day, she could too.

These descriptions of Arjun's bowel movements became

more and more graphic until one day her own imagery ("Today, Arjun did susu five times, and one time it was white, the other time yellow and smelled like old aalu-ghobi") made her throw up. They discovered she was pregnant.

Rakesh took full credit for this, as usual. "I can't believe I did it once with you and—"

But a strange thing happened. Either because he was enamored of his virility, or because he knew Sangita's mother wasn't around to dole out maternal comfort, or because her nipples started to darken and her face began to fill out—Rakesh was suddenly attracted to her.

Sangita thought it was her enlarging breasts. She was certain it was the breasts. That's what he touched and admired first, even before the stomach.

The sexual obsession that followed was financed by a series of power cuts in the muggiest of Octobers, the room so sticky and corrupted by shadows that there was nothing to do but partake in the climate, add to it, *steam things up*, as it were. Rakesh and Sangita went at it from their respective peaks. Everywhere in the bedroom, clothes fluttered to the ground, lay there in troubled piles, the servant was given free tickets to the movie, outside a shawl seller put the full weight of his body into the doorbell, and still the only sound inside was that of a strange hatching, the stripping of Sangita from sexless to sexy, the shrilling of the doorbell (the power was back) like a kettle you purposely choose to not turn off, the water lost to evaporation, the cool drying after you have made love. She lay on her back, glistening. She lay on her side, watching. His hands around her, a spastic garland for her stomach that she could shrug off any second. Replace with a tantrum. Kick and sob like the baby inside her. But then Rakesh, naked, would stand on the bed to step over her, his head about to be lopped off by the ceiling fan, his foot askance on her rounded stomach, pressing down as if prodding for life—was he going to crush the baby? Was he going to erase the proof of love she carried inside her? Why was he asking for the baby's name? His foot was a crab on the swept beachhead of her stomach. This suspense sent tingles all the way to the far posts of her body: the Vs of her toes, the reddening tip of her chin, the cove of the back. This suspense was a series of hard twitches leading up Rakesh's thigh. This suspense always ended (they were back in bed again, his hands on her swollen ankles) in sex.

Arjun was still too young to open the door.

Mrs. Ahuja had never been happier. She soon gave birth.

The pregnancy and birth had been surprisingly painless (no morning sickness, a peculiar craving for grapes), but seeing the baby utterly depressed her: he looked like a jaded movie star that had emerged on a short smoke-break from the womb. He was brown and had a wrinkly forehead. The name *Varun* she picked because it was the closest she could get to the name *Arjun* without picking *Arun*, which was too close.

Her depression was alleviated slightly when people came to greet them from all over Delhi. She took deep pleasure in Rakesh's praise ("she was so relaxed the whole time, such a good wife"), and in the guests' compliments, and in the way

Rakesh chatted and hooted ("Yograj saahb! How is the good wife!") with men he'd claimed to hate with all his pent-up vindictiveness ("If you ever read Yograj has been murdered, tell the police to put a warrant out in my name."). He was incapable of being vicious in person, it seemed. His imagination was violent, that was all, and his constant failure to transform this into a threatening personality is what made him irritable: Sangita finally understood.

After all the people had left, Rakesh said, "I have a surprise for you, darling. Just wait."

Sangita hoped it was her mother. She hadn't heard from her parents since her marriage and had finally broken down and written them a heartbreaking letter describing how she was a maid in the house and then scrunched up that letter and posted another one that stated she was "very happy."

Now she wished nothing more than for her mother to see the truth in this statement.

Rakesh led an elderly lady into the bedroom. "This is Rashmi's mother," he said.

An awful deal was then foisted upon Sangita. She was to call Rashmi's mother "Mama," and allow her to be the children's grandmother, their Nani. What would Sangita get out of it? A kind foster mother and support in bringing up the children.

Rakesh seemed to see the cruelty of this arrangement because that night in bed he started sharing with her for the first time his feelings for Rashmi. "Sangita, it was very sad. I loved her very much, and then one morning I woke up and she wasn't there anymore. For many months I thought: If we had parked the car differently, if I had not been arguing with her on that day, it would not have happened. You understand? Thank you for being in my life."

Apparently, he didn't see the cruelty of talking about Rashmi.

This was when Sangita decided it wasn't worth her time to chase after her husband's affection; he'd never stopped grieving, and maybe he never would. She focused instead on Arjun. She needed to win Arjun's love before he found out she was a stepmother. They were already so close. He was her chief adviser, her calm Rasputin, her deputy prime minister, her ardent bureaucrat—already a mature six while Varun bamboozled his way through his twos. Arjun helped her so much. Together, they tackled crucial questions: How to watch a lot of TV *and* not get sick *and* not have the house overrun by hordes of infants trying to teethe their way into every corner? How to keep the house compartmentalized into air-conditioned pockets, the doors hammered tight, no baby's screams lost in the moats of hot air stagnating between rooms? And when Rakesh requested his children to roam the garden outside during one of his large political functions, introducing them to every dignitary, how would she keep them from dropping Cola bombs on the grass below, having their suits laundered with grime, plowing the lawn to fallowness with their heels?

But Rakesh, who only saw his children on their best behavior, a few hours in the day, didn't want Arjun to be a wetnurse. He didn't understand the sheer necessity. "He is eleven now; he should be playing sports with the other children in the colony," he'd say, producing a cricket bat from behind his back.

But Arjun had no talent for sports; he always ended up being the umpire.

"Here, Arjun, here are some novels."

But the Wodehouses and Christies went unread, their pages improvised as bibs.

"Arjun, why don't you come with me to a party?"

But Arjun wouldn't be comfortable until he had at least three younger siblings to order around and collectively corner the waiters who never otherwise served snacks or drinks to children.

Sangita felt proud that she knew her eldest son—her son!—and his obsession with crowds so well, so much so that she didn't mind when Rakesh scolded her for "turning him into a maid" and "teaching him nothing" and certainly didn't care that Arjun was far more spoiled than the other children, given more food, given better birthday presents, he was the oldest by four years—how could he not be spoiled?

There was another upshot to this excess attention from Mr. Ahuja: Arjun became a brat. He started standing up to his father. When Mr. Ahuja commanded him to do his homework, Arjun would snap back at him and sulk. When Mr. Ahuja asked Arjun to meet an important guest on the verandah, Arjun would settle in front of the TV and play video-games. There was no telling what Arjun would get away with next.

Rakesh was bewildered. No one ever spoke back to him. Lacking anyone else to blame, he blamed Sangita.

"I'm going to tell him," Rakesh said one day, out of the blue. "I'm going to tell him about his mother."

He hadn't brought this up in five years, and Sangita panicked. She thought she could bargain her way out with sex. They now had nine children and zero privacy; they'd reverted from sex to fondling—yes, when was the last time they had made love? It was late at night in the nursery, the children were asleep, and Sangita innovated. She rose from the mat, went from cot to cot and shoved each one with her hips, so that the babies inside swung to wakefulness. They turned on their tiny fleshy backs and began a tirade of shrieking and mewling. One baby screamed, then another opened its eyes, then the whole nursery was screaming, wails rising through the room in perfect nocturnal synchronicity. She knew her older children well: they'd never wake up in the middle of the night to soothe the babies. She waited for Rakesh to reach for her. He stood from her across the room, surveying the scene like he had no role in its creation, like he was there for the first time—and panicking. She returned to the mat near the TV and waited. Slowly he started to make his way through the aisles, treading delicately, as if a false move would, through some inversion of the processes of the universe, put the screaming babies to sleep and ruin the moment. Then he couldn't hold himself back: he came hurtling toward her.

But the satisfaction of sex—that strange, noisy lovemaking camouflaged by the wails of babies—didn't change him. Again in the morning he said, "I'm going to tell him."

• • •

This time Sangita took the threat seriously. She backed off from her son. She cut him off from all his baby-watching responsibilities. She followed Rakesh's orders and untethered twelve-year-old Arjun from the family tree, the distance between Arjun and his family growing like his upwardly-mobile height-markings on the bathroom wall, his afternoons spent in the fluorescent bask of tennis courts or sharing saliva with the general populace in the Gymkhana Club Swimming Pool, his homework hot and ready on his desk when he got home, no time to shower, only the dampness of underarms as he pressed his pen to paper and knew nothing, adjusted his shorts, squeezed his legs, felt a decade-old itch in his pelvis. Of course, he was terrible at tennis and always came back from the pool complaining that someone had accidentally dived onto him while he did a lap, and the only thing good that came out of his free time was the question:

Mama. How do you and Papa have babies? Was Varun in your stomach for four years? Do you have a baby by living with someone for many years?

He'd follow Sangita around asking that question, and she'd say, *Why don't you ask your Papa?* But she knew Papa was only good for banalities, for sugar-coated rhetoric, for promises he couldn't keep (she imagined him saying: *I must thank the people—the people!—for making my wife pregnant.*), that the relationship between mother and father and children was such that the children learned everything valuable from the mother and pretended to be grown-up and competent before the father.

But she ignored Arjun now. It broke her heart to be short and curt with him when he tried to help, but she felt their relationship would only worsen if he knew she wasn't even his real mother. After all these years and a dozen children, she still felt unworthy of love.

So she threw herself into the organizational problems of managing her children. She used delegation. Divide and rule. Even terror. She sent the girls on elaborate spying missions (What does the maid eat when I am not looking? Which baby needs new diapers?) payable entirely in TV-viewing-time. She was all but powerless without the Cartoon Network, her favorite mode of bribery. It was almost fun.

Then news came from Dalhousie that Sangita's mother had passed away.

Sangita was devastated. Lacking love from Rakesh and Arjun—the two people who could most have validated her existence because they actually owed her nothing by blood—she had secretly started obsessing about inviting her mother to marvel at her life. She wanted to show her controlling Mummy what she'd become. Her whole life had been a performance for her mother, and now her mother had skipped out on the show.

Sangita's domestic routine became utterly pointless. She took pleasure in nothing. She spent days at a stretch watching TV. She saw her brood for what it was: a messy constituency that supported Rakesh endlessly. She became obsessed with the hit series titled *The Vengeful Daughter-in-Law*. She stopped gorging herself on mangoes, as was her habit during a pregnancy. She submitted to sex in the nursery with a dreary uninterested look on her face; even the risk of being caught didn't turn her on.

And when Rakesh scolded her about Arjun's poor marks in school, she simply said, "Please tell him."

"Tell who?" said Rakesh, smacking a curtain. "Tell the servant to make tea? Tell the postman to get post? Tell the baby to drink milk? Sangita, you are always using pronouns. Tell what? Tell who?"

"Please tell him," she said. "Tell Arjun about me. About his real mother."

"No," he said.

Finally, Rakesh was so frustrated that he took her to the doctor.

The doctor did what he always did. He pleaded that she not have this child, Sangita's twelfth. The risk of Down syndrome increased with every child, and there was a good chance this baby would be somehow damaged, malformed.

Rakesh said to her in the car, "We can stop this one if you want. I am sorry."

"No," she said.

"You're very brave," he said, with a sigh.

Yes. She had no shortage of bravery.

Was this why she felt no shame when Arjun walked in on them? Was this why she'd practically let it happen?

They were on the floor of the nursery, late at night. All the children were asleep, and she could hear all the creaky sounds of the evening as Rakesh lay on top of her and undid the strings of her pajamas, as he moved his hand all over her stomach and said, "It's okay, Sangita, it's okay," she could hear everything—the start-stop almost-fake screaming of the babies, newborn larynxes vibrating in newborn bodies, the way the cots always swayed at once, the fan overhead screwing itself off the ceiling, even the soft plop of his erect penis against his stomach after he slipped off his own pants. But this particular night there was another sound: the creaking of a door, footsteps. She could have warned Rakesh, she could have quickly forced him to roll off, but she didn't, why didn't she?

He couldn't hear anything except his own panting.

Then Arjun opened the door and let out a brief exclamation. It was too late. Rakesh rolled off her abruptly, ashamed. He glared into the space above Arjun's head. Sangita recognized that look instantly—she remembered it from the first night of her marriage, the way his face throbbed uncertainly between pity and revenge, as if there was no difference between the two. She knew that something was about to give for good, just as she had known then. She knew something was coming to an end, and yet she could not get bring herself to panic. Arjun had seen everything, he had retreated into the hollows of the house, and Rakesh was still glaring at the doorway, frozen over her, on his four limbs, head twisted backward terribly, like an animal. But didn't it have to happen sometime? Hadn't she told him so many times, for months, we are taking a risk, we can't keep doing this, someone will find out?

Yes, a part of her wished that she could have shared her husband's shame, that she could have gathered him up to her bosom and soothed him like a child. But right then, all she could feel was relief. As she saw the exasperation bloom on Rakesh's face, all she could think was *Yes, finally, he has found someone else to blame.*

CHAPTER 12

A FLYOVER, FINALLY

IT WAS SIX FORTY-FIVE IN THE EVENING when the four boys began to descend the flyover.

Earlier, they had left the GK Barista and discussed the possibility of finding a new practice space. They cruised along the same route Arjun had traversed in the school bus; the unreeling landscape reminded him of Aarti, he could string together the succulent sentences of their conversation with every gnarled tree, the traffic lights that flickered neurotically between red and yellow, the large tracts of Chinese restaurants hunched together under large dragon-toting billboards, and when they passed the mysterious, incomplete Godse Nagar Flyover, Arjun asked Ravi to slow down. The two slopes of the flyover ended in midair, never touching. A number of daunting construction machines—grinders, lifters, mixers—dozed under the flyover. The car halted at the red light, and Arjun rolled down his window. "Here," he shouted.

Ravi killed the car skeptically. The in-progress Godse Nagar Flyover—particularly its exposed underside—was hardly a grand specimen. The structure was held aloft by a series of twin columns and arches shaped like upturned boats. Ugly beards of dust hung from the ceiling, and the entire complex—the orange fence, the small buzzcut palms, the crumbling floor tiles, the scabs of B-movie posters stuck on the columns—was burnished with a thin layer of soot that glowed in the high beams of the capsizing sun. The setting was serene: two beggars lay about on gray mats, a child nursed at a young woman's breast, an old man stared angrily from a tent, perhaps contemplating the rivulets of water pronging out through the dust and despairing that the daytime sprinkler had been shut off. Barring the noise—the thousands of ballooned souls bursting out of their vehicles with crazed honks—this could have been the reddened surface of Mars.

Arjun cleared the two rusty MEN AT WORK signs at the base of the flyover. He wiped his hands on his jeans. Then he began walking slowly to the very top of the flyover, Ravi breathing very loudly as he followed, now extremely conscious of the bony pedals and shifts that kept one's body earthbound, Arjun urging him to keep going, their feet gripping the fresh road with a sense of desperation. There were no protective barriers on the side. In a matter of minutes, they were at the top, fifty feet in the air, the road giving way to long rods of steel ahead of them, the lights illuminating a patch of nothingness that hung between the two ends of the incomplete road. Ravi held a girder and gasped. Anurag whooped from behind them.

Arjun tread softly on the fresh tar. “My father built this,” he whispered to Ravi.

“You’re crazy,” said Ravi.

To demonstrate that Ravi was, in fact, correct in his diagnosis, Arjun walked to the very end of the road and stood there, a single inch of road separating the tips of his shoes from total darkness. Then he kicked, he kicked furiously, he didn’t know why, he couldn’t possibly, and there started a rain of rubble from the parapet and Arjun drew back fearfully on his heels, the April air whispering around him with an unexpected coolness, and there was a singular upthrust from the cavity, and he saw it then: a flock of pigeons nesting at the very end of the iron rods had been shoved into sudden flight, the birds were nosediving into the muddy hollow below before floating out from under the flyover, all dust and wings. The rubble had wings! He turned back to the band and faced the boys. They stared back. This was the first time they had viewed him with a measure of awe (it wouldn’t last long).

“Get the guitars out,” he said.

They did, gathering around Arjun in a semicircle while Ravi used a discarded metal board for percussion. And then, immersed in this personal drama, Arjun turned his back to the cavity and sang. He bellowed with exaggerated passion from the top of the flyover; and the pools of individual thoughts—those chambers in his head that vibrated at odds—seemed to connect through the complex system of his vocal pipes, so that at the moment he hit the highest note, he was either all thought or all vacuum (all vacuum, generally), and the note had the quality of the first leak in a massive dam, terrifying because it promised much worse. But it didn't matter. He couldn't care what anyone thought at that moment. He was singing, drawing sound from all the silent orifices of his body the way a heart draws blood, physically evoking the melody of "Living on a Prayer" without a lyric sheet or a sense of the original tune, doing it with nothing, no microphone, no electric guitars, just, as he would like to say years later, Arjun Ahuja Unplugged. It was at that moment that he was finally free of Aarti, a mixture of fear and confidence overtaking his body. It was the way he would feel when he had sex for the first time, somehow forgetting the girl, her name, her face—overcome by a drastic implosion of his own senses as he tried to pretend it was all right, this wasn't the end, he'd be fine.

He turned his back to his band and sang into the gap. Then he stopped abruptly and let the music clang on without him in an endless outro. He had had a vision. For a brief instant, the instant before he stopped midsentence, he had imagined Mr. Ahuja driving up on the opposite slope of the flyover and letting his Toyota Qualis creak menacingly at the precipice, the lights of the vehicle floodlighting the band as the eight children huddled inside screamed with delight—those children that were his audience, his fans, his dire siblings. The family at its most pleasant: watching from a distance while you sank into yourself, you imploded, you were finally alive.

CHAPTER 13

CROWD SURFING

THE FOUR BOYS LEAPED INTO THE CAR with a newfound sense of camaraderie: Ravi giddyupping his Hyundai Santro with abrupt gear shifts; Anurag in the passenger seat with his elbow dangerously V-ed out of the car; and Deepak persisting in looking dopey and bemused beside Arjun. All of them were under age and illegal; driving age was eighteen. They filed into an endless queue of cars, rolled the windows down, joined the slow pilgrimage to lung cancer.

Arjun was in a grand mood now. He tapped Ravi on the shoulder and said, "Yaar—none of this shorts-wearing business when we do a concert, okay? No one wants to see your hairy legs, understood? We'll wear black. Since we are dark.

Let's all wear black pants. And maybe we can have our pockets pulled out?" He demonstrated. "See? Looks kind of cool, yeah? Every band has to have a specific fashion style. Bono has those fundoo shades. Metallica has leather. Shania Twain has a belly button."

"She also has a pussy," Anurag noted. "That I was—"

"You too?" asked Deepak, solicitously. "She has no self-respect or what."

Arjun shushed them. "Shut up, you idiots. Are you listening? Pockets should be out. It looks like your legs have ears. Or your hips are shitting."

"Since when have *you* started protecting Shania, yaar," asked Anurag in his slow drawl. "What is she to you—a sister?"

"Good job singing Bryan Adams," Ravi muttered. "Did you know Shania Twain and your lovely Bryan Adams have the same producer? And that Shania is married to that producer? Shania banged by Mutt Lange."

Such lascivious recounting of rock history was a strange counterpoint to the utterly sexless action unfolding on the other side of Ring Road as they approached the Moolchand Flyover. All four boys turned to look. Three huge flanks of sari and salwar-kameez-clad women—there must have been at least fifty in all—were milling about excitedly as if at a Saturday bazaar; huge spurts of dust jetted up from around their legs into the awfully dry April evening. The concentration of women was particularly dense under the lone laburnum tree by the road side, its yellow flowers burning brightly overhead in some sort of twilight vigil. A slight parting of their bodies revealed a giant portrait of a young rosy-cheeked man. It was propped against the trunk of the laburnum. The women approached one by one, bent their covered heads with respect, and then carefully strung garlands of marigolds around the frame.

The other ladies sang and beat their chests and shed fat tears on the sidewalk.

Anurag rolled down his window and hooted.

"Don't do that, duffer," said Deepak.

"Someone important died or what?" said Anurag.

"You're an idiot man," said Deepak. "Even if it's not important. You hoot when someone dies?"

Arjun shrugged. "That TV star died, yaar. Mohan Bedi, yaar. I think it's him."

"Who the hell is Mohan Bedi?" Ravi asked.

The answer came in the form of a neck-breakingly sudden lurch of the car, both Ravi and Anurag thrown headfirst (they weren't wearing seat belts, were too manly for that) into the windscreen while Arjun and Deepak spilled forward into a fetal crouch, the four boys' heads already aching from what they'd seen: a girl, some girl, hitting the front of the car and literally *flying*—arms and legs propellered in a blur around her—ten feet from the island on which she'd been standing before she mistakenly stepped out onto the main road. Luckily, as she lay on the ground, her purse and cell phone thud-thud-thudding on the road beyond, no cars sped ahead to finish the job. It was rush hour and miraculously no vehicles were coming her way. Ravi had braked just in time. This had saved him from cracking his skull; ditto Anurag. They got out of the Santro with hands massaging their own necks. The road was hot and bloodless: the girl wasn't bleeding! She was their age, Arjun noticed as he stepped out of the car. She was lying on her back, her jeans torn, scooterists dodging around her broomlike hair—but she wasn't bleeding! Everyone, Arjun included, was approaching the girl with the absurd plea of *shit shit shit*. Hello, dying person, shit shit shit! He didn't even notice that all the men and women on the other side of the road had rushed over and that he, Arjun, was about to be flattened in a stampede of Jurassic Park proportions. He was jostled out of the way. The girl was surged forward like a crowd-surfer in a concert; a hundred hands off-loaded her onto the sidewalk, two other hands, someone's charitable hands, laid her purse and cell phone next to her. This was a poor country, but people would astound you again and again with their lack of greed: Arjun and Ravi and Anurag and Deepak, richie-rich, young, so central to the tragedy, had become spectators.

They were standing on Ring Road with five cars honking at them, asking them to move, *what are you doing, please move your Santro, do you realize it's in the middle of the road?* In fact, Arjun *did*, and he was transfixed by the thought that for every second he stood on Ring Road like a fucking stooge, the delay was sending spasms backward all through the city, igniting tempers at traffic lights, so that when a man left work at six o'clock to return to his wife, son, daughter, it would take him an hour longer than usual—an hour in which anything could happen—you could lose someone you loved, vital organs could fail. But the girl wasn't dead.

Nor was she okay. She was a terrifying in-between: conscious, half-sitting up, palms dusty, still sobbing, she had a puffed-up face. Death or serious injury to the girl would have meant bodily harm for the boys; the crowd, poor and understandably resentful to begin with, would have played out some form of street justice, berating them, lynching them from the parapet of a flyover (or so Arjun imagined). But the women who were cradling the girl in their arms were mothers. They were fans of *The Vengeful Daughter-in-Law*, the TV show. They felt a mixture of maternal warmth and anger toward the girl: *What were you thinking crossing the road like this, are you okay, don't cry darling, promise you'll never do anything like this again?* They understood that she needed a doctor immediately. They agreed to let the four boys take her to Moolchand Hospital five minutes away.

Arjun had never held a crying girl before—not one of this age. She lay in a zigzag of limbs across Anurag's and Arjun's laps in the car, weeping, dripping snot. Arjun shushed and soothed her like she was a baby.

Ravi, in the front, kept talking. "Shit, we're finished. Shit. I can't tell my dad. He'll kill me. I don't want to go to jail. Shit."

"Shut up, man," said Arjun. "You have to call him. She's crying. We'll worry later." He looked at the girl. "Are you okay?"

"You okay, sweety?" Anurag asked.

"Sweety? Shut up, Anu."

CHAPTER 14

DIWAAN-E-KHAAS

Mr. Ahuja stood in the Super Prime Minister's drawing room—still hot and smoky from a religious ceremony—and carefully studied Rupa Bhalla's body language as she signaled him into an uncomfortable cane chair with a swish of her saffron dupatta. She was shaped like one of those rolled mattresses you saw people resting on at railway stations—highly unstable, giving, when she walked, the general impression of being pushed—and she sat down on a maroon chair with a palpable sense of relief. Then, without pause, she commanded him to drink a lassi, asked him what type of lassi he liked, shouted for the servant, said she knew he liked namkeen from the wedding they'd been to—

what did Rakesh think, had she planned the wedding well?—but right now the type of lassi escaped her, it was namkeen, was it not?

Rakesh was immediately on guard. He told her the wedding was corrupt, ostentatious, theatrical.

She laughed and said, "Thank you."

Still, she was being formal, distant. She'd not once asked him about his family—as was her habit—and now she was pretending to forget what type of lassi he liked.

This was absurd. The whole country knew he drank kesar.

"I'd like namkeen, yes, you're right," demurred Rakesh. "So, ji, I've come to explain my letter—"

Rupa looked relieved. "I'm so glad," she said, slapping her forehead theatrically. "I thought you had *also* come to resign!"

He protested, "Rupa-ji, but I am *already* resigned. I came to talk about that only."

"*Resigned?*" she said, practically sneezing the word. "Oh yes! Quite right." She tapped her head. "Rohini told me there was an e-mail from you. How was I to know it was a resignation? If she had told me, I would have seen first thing, baba. But e-mail otherwise is just e-mail. These days even I am getting so much spam. Do you know how to get rid of this spam?"

Her mouth a nest of baby sparrows, her voice was that of a schoolgirl. Her large red bindi—that all-knowing dot—had today been replaced by an oily tilak. She leaned across the table for a silver napkin holder, pushing in the yellow triangular fins of paper so they didn't crackle in the fan blast. She talked to people as if their faces were the receivers on a phone apparatus, keeping you so close that you could smell the soft ticking of supari in her mouth, her wicked smile dripping from the corners of her lips like a retired comedian's, eyes nosed so far apart you couldn't look her in both at once.

Rakesh was grateful for the table separating them.

"You said you thought I had come to resign *also*, ji," he said, crossing his legs and rocking the shell of the white cane chair around him. "Who else has resigned?"

"Well," said Rupa, snaking her head from side to side. "A wonderful question! A timely one!"

"Yes?"

"Everyone in our dear party! Except you," she said, clapping her hands for the servant.

"But, ji—that is what I am saying—I am resigned also!"

They had a hearty laugh about this.

"Quite right, quite right," said Rupa, looking distractedly at the door to the kitchen. "Krishan! Bring saahb the lassi! Hen-ji. Sorry. Why are you resigning again?"

"Beg pardon? Find *them*? Find whom?"

"Eh?"

"Eh?"

This misunderstanding afforded a five-second cliffhanger of silence. Both Rupa and Rakesh sat up erect. Rakesh was still coming to terms with the news of this mass resignation and, worse, with the fact that Rupa's state of agitation wasn't simply a result of his visit. To be a minister, after all, was to be the center of a universe frothy with favors and flattery—everywhere you turned were Black Cat Guards, lackeys, peons, CEOs, special interests, undercover journalists—but with Rakesh the feeling of centrality had become particularly acute, nerve-wracking. Indeed, since last night the universe seemed to have telescoped down to a point in his head; a third marble of sadness rolled behind his eyes. Everywhere he looked were signs of his own impending doom—signs he'd first noticed when he and Arjun drove out at twelve at night on Arjun's sixteenth birthday, Rakesh in the driver's seat, Arjun beside him, their Toyota Qualis flying through the carbon-dioxide exhaling green belt of Delhi past the convoyed trucks and the shivering beggars to the first grand site of a flyover, a piece of cordoned road filled simply with Roman-looking columns of concrete and jutting steel, and between the columns coal-faced men carrying bucket after bucket of stone to dump into the foundational pit, a huge chugging grinder behind the men belching gray fumes against the black night, and then rain, rain outlining the shape of the city with its sound, father and son sitting in the car ten feet away, Rakesh trying to tell Arjun, *Always think of the little people behind the grand things*, why was this his message of choice? How had he mistakenly imagined this was Arjun's seventeenth birthday? But what he really wanted to say was, *Think of me, I love you*, and then Arjun had opened the window and diagonal after diagonal of rain came splashing into their laps, and Rakesh knew: Arjun wasn't listening. Arjun was a child in an adult world. Arjun didn't care for his father's political or philosophical tracts; they only had the instinctive bond that parent and child shared.

So Rakesh had no choice but to keep everything at arm's length to protect his son, to take the world by its axis and stab it into his own heart. And when Arjun had walked in on him last night, he'd given up the one secret besides Rashmi he'd managed to keep.

The world's axis turned another notch into his chest. The pressure in his sinuses was immense.

"My resignation of course is a different subject—" sniffed Rakesh.

"Of course your resignation is different!" said Rupa, embargoing a yawn with her hand. "That's because you are educated and from a good family and all that, and you wouldn't resign over something so foolish. You know, none of these menfolk who are so happily resigning today have even *watched* the show. If you ask me: very stupid, it is. Firstly, no one would care if a virtuous *woman* on TV died, isn't it? Maybe Tulsi, but no one else. You know how this sexism-vexism is. Secondly, what makes me more angry, actually, is that all these *women* are asking that he be brought back! Otherwise, there will be a strike today! All over India! The three and a half cheeks of it!"

A show? Rakesh thought. *A TV show?*

The three and a half cheeks of it?

"Did you know," Rupa continued, "that the resignation letters I have in my possession at the present moment were written by the wives of our good MPs and ministers? What is wrong with these menfolk, tell me? And because their wives—not them—have written the letters, they are all saying, if you don't make Mohan Bedi return to the show, we will seek your resignation! Imagine! Super Prime Minister isn't even a real post, and they want to kill it."

Rupa chortled and Rakesh winced. He still had no idea what Rupa was talking about. If he had listened to his wife even once when they went about their rare joint tasks—containing a mushroom cloud of shit blooming in a two-year-old's diaper, floating side-by-side the soft pontoons of the babies in a bathing bucket, carefully labeling each milk bottle in the fridge—he would have known not only the name of the TV show *The Vengeful Daughter-in-Law* but also the life-story, dental history, constipation woes, and general meal-size of the fictitious Bedi family.

But he never listened to her; he hated her mindless entertainments; all he carried in his mind was the first hint of familiarity. Mohan Bedi was a known name and an unknown quantity.

Even that was okay: what truly annoyed Mr. Ahuja was that no one in his party had bothered informing him about the mass resignation. Yes: why hadn't *anyone* told him? He felt abandoned, sidelined, out of the loop, betrayed. He *did* think of his colleagues as family—so intensely in fact that his alienation was that of an adolescent. Overfamiliarity was the only way Rakesh knew to make friends; he was as deeply personal in friendship as he was in revenge. It had begun when he had told the SPM: *Look, my children don't have anyone except their parents. My whole family is gone. I was an only child. My father was an only child. No grandparents on either side. They love you. They want you to be their Dadi.* Over time, the children had become a cult; Rakesh's party had become a family. Governors and chief ministers and party secretaries and freedom fighters and judges were known not by name but by their prefixes: Mama, Mami, Dada, Dadi, Chacha, Chachi, Taiji, so on. They appeared at the children's birthdays, liquored up, twisting their cake-drenched paper plates into half-moons, kicking up divots of grass with their sharp-heeled slippers, sweating till they were desiccated into shadows. They made fools of themselves with baby-talk. You saw in their eyes their own loneliness—how they had come all the way to Delhi to rule the country and left behind their families, their people in distant villages.

How many times had he stormed a stuffy politician with the light brigade of his children, their hands all falling at the respected elder's feet in veneration? How many times had he left in the middle of an embarrassing meeting, citing the outbreak of a minor epidemic in his house? How many times had his children smuggled in chocolates for a politician on a hunger strike?

He'd fix them. He'd make a grab for power.

"Rupa-ji, I would never resign over something so petty, as you know. I think this is absurd. I have stood apart from the party with a very pointed purpose. However, I too have needs.

I too have one request: suspend Yograj. He has been interfering with the Flyover Fast-Track on all levels. Please consider my letter and suspend him."

"Arre, Ahuja. I can't simply accept Vineet's resignation at the moment," Rupa said. "He's holding this entire stupid opposition to me together."

"Very well then, Rupa-ji. I respect your decision even as I disagree with it. I hope you know I am hundred percent behind you on the issue of the mass resignation. We can talk about Vineet when things calm down."

It was only when Rakesh walked out, waved to his driver, watched a renegade wind slap up a curtain of dust that then went sailing right *into* his beleaguered nostrils, that he took a sneeze out of his day to congratulate himself. He had Rupa in his pocket. All he had to do now was confront his party members.

CHAPTER 15

BACKHANDED COMPLIMENTS

THUS, AT THE MEETING OF PAY SCALES—where thirteen "resigned" Members of Parliament were in attendance around a beveled table—Rakesh made his displeasure clear. "Why did the news of this so-called mass resignation come to me so late, please tell me? I know there is this impression I am *personally* building each flyover by hand and that all thirteen of my children are operating the machinery and that I must not be disturbed, but you know, even an artist like me must be fully immersed in the real world. There are a thousand ways for me to be reached. One can try one of the twelve cell phones my staff has. Even buggers, low-ranked IAS buggers can reach me. Then there are a thousand pigeons that migrate between my office and my house. One can tie a locket around one of their green necks. One can e-mail me. You can even call up and tell my children. So?"

The enormous difficulty of delivering such a speech was best highlighted by the number of times cell phones rang and were answered during its delivery: nine.

Unfortunately, the first person to respond was none other than Rakesh's famed nemesis and favored resignation subject, Vineet Yograj. "Where were you at five o'clock? Yesterday?" Yograj asked in his eager, friendly, gruff manner. He was a man with a teak-dark face and an onion-shaped white goatee who was renowned for grilling anyone he met. "You are very busy with Flyover Fast-Track correct? Working overtime? No time for us these days, Rakesh-ji?"

Rakesh puffed out his chest and said, "Vineet-saahb has thrown open the proceedings with his trademark interrogation. Anyone else?"

"But Rakesh-ji, why were you not at the cabinet meeting?" said Vineet, unfazed. He was sitting two seats to Rakesh's right. He opened his clenched fists. "Before I forget! I have brought cardamom for all of you. Please take some. I've bought it fresh from Kerela. It has great medicinal value."

Vineet's ploy paid off. The female MPs across the table leaned toward him, thus affording him a better view of their bloused breasts as he rolled the green pods of cardamom into their outstretched hands. The transaction thus completed, the pods were passed around the table. Only Rakesh pulled back stiffly into his seat and said with a smirk, "No thank you, ji.

This is exactly why I don't attend cabinet meetings. God knows what poison Vineet-saahb you will feed us."

"The reason Vineet-ji is asking," said an MP, "is that we reached a consensus after the cabinet meeting only."

"What at the cabinet meeting?" said Rakesh, putting a hand beside his ear. "The bill?"

"No. *Consensus*, ji."

Rakesh slapped the table. "But you weren't even there, Iyenger-saahb."

Iyenger was not a cabinet minister.

"But we met outside the room. After Madam Rupa-ji left. After Madam was out of sight."

"Out of sight, out of mind, isn't it?" said Rakesh. "Apparently, the same thing happened to me. I could not attend the cabinet meeting because I had to talk to a delegation of American planners—what can one do? Such commitments are always there. Now. I have offered my excuse. What about you? Why didn't I hear?"

He looked threateningly around the room at the junior MPs, eyebrows grossly bunched, left hand turning a spoon in his cup of tea so that it sounded like the ringing of a school bell. The sandstone building let in a slice of sun and gust after gust of air. The light—low-density, orange—filled the spaces between men and women, expanded, flamed against the contours of the room so that the Savarkar Room felt to Mr. Ahuja like a dirigible plunged by accident of speed and latitude into perpetual afternoon. Not surprising, then, that Mr. Ahuja—having had a sleepless night—felt tired, jet-lagged, and not at all in the mood for the flattery the junior MPs began dishing out.

One MP said, "According to me, Rakesh-ji, there are two reasons. One is that I thought you would hear eventually—which it seems you did. And two, ji—this is the highest compliment I can give—I think you are above politics. That is why I did not call."

"He is right," said Iyenger. "Nowadays I see you more on STARNews than in Parliament. I thought you will laugh on my face if I said we are resigning for such a silly reason."

"You have become a pukka CEO!" added another. "A technocrat!"

"We are very inspired by your efforts with your ministry."

Rakesh was irritated. To say he was "above politics" was to essentially say he wasn't a good politician. Yes, this was ridiculous: he was being punished now for being an efficient worker? For sweating over infrastructure rather than cultivating contacts? Trembling with anger, he got up and reached to draw the blinds—but as he did, his papers fluttered from the table and an MP whipped her dupatta over her shoulder. He turned around, felt the tubes of his shirtsleeves flute with turbulence. The MPs were holding their cups of tea to their noses; on the table below, ring after ring of condensation startled into a blinding orange, then eclipsed into an even teak. All eyes turned from the wooden tabletop. To him. A familiar and delirious rhythm of saliva and silence percolated in his throat. His hands flattened on the paper; he leaned in to the crowd of gray heads—the perfect posture for a lambasting session. "I wasn't at the cabinet meeting, but I am here now, naah?" said Rakesh, holding his palm up. "You people talk such nonsense. Luckily, I am as foolish as all of you people. I have also resigned."

The round of repartees was jovial. Again, he felt triumphant. They'd accused him of not being enough of a politician, and he'd hit back with a fantastic backhand, a googly, a double play. Now they thought he'd joined *their* ranks for the cause of Mohan Bedi, and Rupa Bhalla thought he was 100 percent behind her. He'd covered both bases.

"Okay," said Rakesh, snorting, "let us get down to business."

But when the agenda was being passed around, Vineet asked Rakesh, "Accha, ji. Where did you buy this stylish shirt from?"

"Gift," said Rakesh.

"The tie?"

"Inherited."

"Jacket?"

"Borrowed."

(The other MPs watched this volleying, extremely amused.)

"Borrowed? From whom?" inquired Yograj, politeness itself.

"What did you just say? Anyway. Please let us get on with business."

"But you didn't tell," said Vineet. "How did you hear of the resignation?"

"You'll have to speak up."

"HOW DID YOU HEAR?"

"Well. You *are* shouting! That is how."

"You are pulling my leg. How did you hear about the resignation?"

"Sources."

Vineet said. "I hear you visited Madam today?"

"To resign, why else?"

"Look," said Vineet, turning to the other MPs, "I told you Rakesh-ji is having great inner strength. He must be having the flaxseeds I gave last time. None of us others resigned in person."

"Yes. How was she?" they asked. "What did she say?"

"Come again?"

"HOW WAS SHE?"

"Angry," Rakesh snorted. "She said she was going to suspend most of you. I had to convince her not to, even as I myself was resigning! I think madam realized that I was the final nail in the coffin. How many people can she suspend?" Then he added, "You people should be happy I was there at the right moment."

Well done, Ahuja!

However. The exhilaration of his extemporaneous turncoat lasted only so long: back in the car, on the way to the ministry, the gaps in his teeth nicely irrigated by tea, he was again bothered that no one had updated him about the resignations.

Maybe he *should have* put the buggers in their place—minced no words about how he wanted no part in this TV farce, shown that he was furious that they'd mock his commitment to the flyovers rather than praising it. Then again, that would only make him more unpopular in the party. But what if he already was unpopular in the party—and then Rupa Bhalla found out about his false promise of support? Who would he have on his side then?

There were no easy answers. All the way to the ministry, every cow he saw was a personal affront to him—a shit-covered hurdle for traffic. The street by now—so pristine in the morning—was a study in chaos. The setting sun offered its own ferocious interpretation of events: light shot between the flat metal hoardings on either side like gunfire in an alley; a man loaded five children mass-suicidally onto the back of his scooter; under a crinkled blue tarpaulin a fat policeman hydrated himself with a glass of the filthiest lemon juice, wiping his mustache just as Mr. Ahuja passed.

Closer, the reflection of Mr. Ahuja's wristwatch—its perfect sphere of heat and light—described a parabolic path over the gray-padded ceiling of the car. The streetlights were straight poles with branched lights that looked like the simplistic V-shaped birds his children made in their first crayonic paintings—he would never let his children drive. This much he was clear about. Never mind that Arjun was approaching eighteen. Never mind that Arjun would never respect him. Never mind that Arjun traveled in a DTC bus every day just like the one that was overtaking Mr. Ahuja's *official*, *white*,

Government Lion Embossed License Plate, *Hindustan Motors Millennium-Edition*, *Leather-Seat* Ambassador at a speed sanctioned only by the movie *Speed* and was now breaking every single rule of inertia in order to suddenly halt behind the five-person scooter—the smallest child on the scooter dropping her ice-cream bar and turning around to wipe her fingers on the dirty grille of the bus as it rocked up and down on its shock absorbers.

Mr. Ahuja asked his driver, Mathur, to slap the red official siren atop the car.

"Important meeting, sir?" Mathur asked, leaning out of the car.

"No, yaar, I'm thinking in terms of your sons. Do you want to see them grow up into young men? If this traffic continues, this car will be a coffin by the time you get home."

"Yes, sir, but they will be short—like me," said Mathur, adjusting the pillow he sat on to reach the dashboard. "That is the only thing."

Then the car extruded a massive honk and they were off. Rakesh held his breath.

He tried to see himself through the jaundiced eyes of his colleagues. After all, he'd become what he hated: a complainer, a problem finder. He'd always pooh-poohed Indians who complained about traffic, taking a certain nationalist pride in the open show of might and opportunism, but ever since Rashmi's accident, he'd begun to palpitate over the risks drivers took to slice into the smallest gap, to overtake blindly from the left, the number of dents on even the newest cars, the way a pedestrian was expected to write a fresh will before crossing the road.

The traffic had been the same level of terrible when he and Rashmi came home for their first holiday from Vermont nearly twenty years ago. What had changed was Rashmi. She'd imbibed the straight magical lines of the West, its fetish for sanity. She asked the driver not to run red lights. Rakesh pointed out that this was his Masi's driver, and that we people from USA should not order him around and that *if we don't run this bloody red light we'll be flattened by the angry-looking truck approaching from the right, do you see it?* Rashmi prayed calmly to the driver not to kill the poor man on the rickshaw in front of them. The driver didn't listen. Rashmi said, What is wrong with us Indians? Rakesh took offense, and said, Firstly, speak for yourself, darling, and also, What is wrong with the British that they conquered India and then left us poor and with bad laws and a corrupt civil service and then created schools where we educated people to be engineers and journalists only so that they could leave the country and then live abroad and come back for a few days in the year and say: Oh, look how trickly and toxic the shower is, if I get naked a thousand flies will feast on my body, everybody I touch is like a beggar only—

(He was in a bad mood because he'd argued with his parents.)

She said, You've done it again.

He said, I'm sorry.

You can't just say sorry and think it's over.

I'm so sorry, he said.

The driver heard their argument and laughed. This made Rakesh doubly mad. He said, Let me drive.

Rashmi said, You don't have an Indian license.

Soon Rashmi and Rakesh were sitting in the front. Rakesh was hunched over the steering wheel.

Rashmi said, We Indians believe in fate. Look at these people driving like maniacs. We Indians. Believe in. Fate.

Rakesh said, What fate.

Look at this cow you're about to hit.

Cows believe in fate.

He hit the cow.

Now Rakesh had damaged his Masi's brand-new Contessa (a big cow-shaped dent had formed on its bonnet) and had to bribe the driver.

The driver said, Sir, money you will give me, but what about my job?

We'll say it wasn't your fault, Rashmi said in her sweetest voice.

They sat shamefaced in front of Rakesh's Masi. Already their family relations were strained—Rakesh's mother and Masi were involved in a property dispute—and now Rakesh was going to admit that he'd wrecked her car.

Rashmi said, I did it.

What happened, beta? asked the Masi.

Because I was driving like an American, she said.

Then she gave Rakesh the most short-lived piercing glare possible. She knew how to handle him. She'd won by suddenly making a sacrifice. She was so stunning—with her erect posture and the teasing lilt of her voice, and her hands that sprayed out every which way as she talked—that even his terrifying auntie was charmed. Rakesh, too, could never say anything to Rashmi on the subject of Indian-style driving ever again, and long afterward, in Vermont, he couldn't explain to himself why every mistake a driver made in America felt for him like a minor (guilty) victory; why on the day John the neighbor reversed into their mailbox, he mowed the lawn three times; why when the morning news came in of a nonfatal pileup on the highway, he was strangely ecstatic and cooked rajma like he was a master chef; why on the day Rashmi died, he was aware that if he and Rashmi had been mere spectators of the accident—if it hadn't, in other words, been the day she died—he'd have thrust his hands under the waterfall of her hair, cradled her neck in the confluence of his fingers, and finally told her why he was so happy: she was alive and he had won the argument she'd set into motion on the cow-killing Delhi day two years before. He'd proved that Americans were as prone to bad driving as Indians, that the only difference was that America had police officers and bureaucrats that enforced rules, and Indians had officers with titles like District Magistrate of Jats, Joint Secretary for Tribal Welfare Scheme Attached to the Ministry of Welfare, Inspector of Mining, Collector for the Sub District Falling Between Chhatisgarh and Madhya Pradesh, Director

(Sub) of Special Preservation of Languages whose job was to simply figure out the purpose of these titles.

But he would never have said this. Someone had been run over by a motorcycle and a door was flying. But even if he had said this, who would he have said it to? There was no one to argue with ever again. No one to crumple into at a moment's notice.

Only people to blame.

So when Rakesh returned to India and found himself once again in the country's royal mess, he blamed everything on the administrative service, the police force, the babus, that bureaucratic mess that had rejected *him* and made him flee to the US; that made him fill out ten pages of paperwork in order to transfer Rashmi's ashes to India; that lost the papers; that fined him ten thousand rupees at customs for his "imported Tourister Funeral Urn." And that finally extracted three bribes from him at the airport—bribes Rakesh paid because he didn't want to be late for his wife's fourth-day rites and because he was rich, because he could. You could smell it on him—his American cologne.

But he could also turn his riches against these tormentors: he vowed to track down the two customs officials who'd given him hell, to use every connection at his disposal to end their careers, and that was how he found himself at the doorstep of Rupa Bhalla, a family friend who was a Member of Parliament and the president of the SZP Party. She too was recently widowed: her husband, Ashok Bhalla, a former Prime Minister, had been sown into a field by a terrorist driving an advanced harvester during the spring festival in Punjab.

She and Rakesh talked for a while and she was impressed by his political views and intelligence and his firsthand anti-Americanism. As Rakesh told her the story about the customs officials, she hobbled about madly in front of the rectangular painting that spanned the entire wall of her drawing room. Over time, with smoke and moisture, the painting had blurred into a constant saffron horizon for the befuddled visitor, its human figures—highly impressionistic to begin with—looking more and more like a series of rotten cauliflowers planted in a desert. The painting was horrible, vomit-inducing, and she said she'd painted it herself.

She was standing in front of the painting, and as Rakesh looked, it seemed as if Rupa Bhalla's face was sprouting a hundred nodes on either side, a gallery of self-portraits that were only a little more hideous than the woman before him. He thought then, with a gasp of terror: here was a mannequin of lost sexuality and beauty. You could tell she had been *something* in her youth; he had seen pictures of her next to her late husband—vivacious, head-up, kissable—the sort of girl who, if she had been from Delhi or Bombay, not Haryana, might have smoked ahead of her time. Who might have walked into a hall of men with brash elegance, bangles clinking a bit too much, a splash of cognac perfuming her bare navel. Who made awful paintings. But she carried her loss of energy like a lesson learned, and now the young Rakesh realized that losing sexuality was to finally be forced into a sort of asceticism, to transcend the pettiness of life, a politician who was driven by nothing but a will to remain alive, then to die in public view. To be seen by all—and had by no one. This idea seemed unbearably romantic to him. He still thought he would never remarry. He wanted badly to become a politician as well.

That was when Rupa Bhalla said that she knew the painting was horrible.

Rakesh had said, No, no, it wasn't.

She laughed and said, It's okay. Just listen.

He said it wasn't horrible at all.

She said, You've passed the test. This is my test. Any new party member who is honest with me, I immediately dismiss, anyone who keeps flattering no matter what—them I keep.

You want me in the party? Rakesh said.

Of course, Rupa said. That is the only way I can help you.

And that was fourteen years ago, Rakesh mused, arriving at the office. Fourteen years of being in and out of power, of having made sure those two customs officials had been posted in a caste violence-ridden sector of Bihar. And still his ambition was unchanged. His entire drive in becoming a minister—when he wasn't making anti-American speeches and protesting against multinationals—was to sit atop the vast, damaged machinery of the Indian civil service and use his powers to hammer their cogs back into their service roles. It was as if he'd touched down in Indira Gandhi Airport all those years before and in passing through the X-ray mutated from a Master of Civil Engineering to a Master of Mass Feeling.

And now, when he'd finally achieved that dream by overseeing every single detail of the bloody Flyover Fast-Track he was being accused of not being enough of a politician?

Even though he was the only one with the slightest iota of idealism? Who actually did anything? Who took the smallest bribes?

There was no credence in his party members' views. They were full of shit, cow dung, specifically.

From his office, he promptly called Sankalp Malik, the one minister who'd sat quietly through the Meeting of Pay Scales.

"Look Sankalp," he said, "I am serious. I didn't say anything at the meeting because why should I cause a big scene? I am a low-key sort of person. I keep in shadows. I am the dark horse. But let me tell you this much. I am thinking about withdrawing support and taking a good chunk of this party with me. I am being repeatedly insulted. This is hardly the way to treat a coalition partner."

"Ahuja-ji. I completely understand—"

"But how, HAND-IN-HAND?" said Mr. Ahuja, cracking his wrists on the table.

Sankalp was adamant. "No, no, no. You are mis-understand-ing. It is definitely bad you were not cc-ed on the mass e-mail that was sent to all ministers."

"Vineet sent it, correct? I know what is happening. Believe

me, I know. Personal rivalry is being allowed to interfere with daily functioning."

"Look, Ahuja-ji," said Sankalp, clearing his throat. "If you will allow me to say. I think this is a terrible business that has been meted out. But Vineet did not send the e-mail. Subhash-ji did. And he explained to me why you were not included. I think there is a perception you are too close to the SPM. That anything you are told, you will tell the SPM—"

Rakesh said, "Yes, of course. I am the SPM's lover. I forgot that aspect."

"No. I scolded Subhash-ji! On your behalf!"

"She has given birth to my children."

"Ji, it is not *my* perception but the perception of others."

"Punning like a poet now?" Rakesh said. He'd heard *perception of others* as the *conception of mothers.*

"Han-ji?" asked Sankalp.

"Never mind. Thanks for your help."

Shit. He put the phone down. So there was no doubt whatsoever. He'd made a terrible mistake by handing Rupa the deranged resignation letter (with the Riot Stock Exchange Bill enclosed!), promising her his support over the Mohan Bedi fiasco, then double-crossing her. She was probably tearing up the insulting letter *right now*. Then Rakesh remembered his career-long mantra: *Anyone who keeps flattering no matter what—them I keep*. Yes, that was the key: he needed to find a way to flatter the SPM. He needed to undo all the damage he'd inflicted on himself. He needed to win back the SPM's sympathies. But how?

Should he name his next child after her? That was the sort of thing that flattered Rupa no end. It would bother Mrs. Ahuja too: she had always wanted a baby named, inexplicably, Chintoo—why, she screamed it out during each delivery—and now she'd have to wait. Let her wait. Rakesh was not looking forward to his upcoming term of cohabitual celibacy with her either. The next six months he would have to watch Sangita's body dome into a temple of Ahuja worship, the breasts suspended like twin bells that you ring upon entering a shrine, but he would be stopped at the threshold, shamed by Arjun. He'd sit outside on the bed, begging for arms—just to be held. Sangita would look away, cold, while his children discussed their father's lust between bouts of homework. In his abdomen he felt the tug of a dead muscle.

"Sir!" said Sunil Kumar.

"Yes? What is the matter? What happened? What happened?"

"I told you I am burning that wasp's nest!"

So that was the smell that had been keeping him awake. So that was the vague directive Sunil Kumar had issued minutes before, gesticulating out of the window. Mr. Ahuja had assumed it was something to do with the wiper-slashes of pigeon shit on his window, a problem Mr. Ahuja always solved by simply leaving the window open, which in turn sent Sunil into geometrical raptures about the exact angle at which a bird would have to excrete in order to hit Mr. Ahuja's ministerial desk dead-center.

Now a huge gust of orange buzzed through the window: wasps tornadoed around curls of smoke. Mr. Ahuja shielded his head in panic—*close the window!*—and Sunil Kumar freed a square of fluorescent light onto the ceiling by flinging open the top of the photocopier. The wasps (moving always in regressive spirals, as if pushing against wind) descended hungrily on the flashing plasma of the photocopier and were instantly squashed as Sunil Kumar clapped the white flap down on their bodies. Seconds later, a white sheet of paper speckled with crushed exoskeletons emerged with a satisfying whirr from the machine. Sunil Kumar grabbed the evidence, made for the door, held it open for Mr. Ahuja, and both of them panted into the corridor—unharmed.

"SUNIL! This is hardly a time to do these things. You know I am getting late—does this have to be done today?"

"Sir, forgive me—the wasps were making this their headquarters too. Sometime I had to kill them. I got on a ladder when you were resigned and burned them. So long it has still taken. Can you imagine? The bastards were sitting inside even as it was burning . . ."

Mr. Ahuja wasn't listening and couldn't hear anyway. From the large bay windows of the corridor, he was aware of a sound that had a much lower register than the collective buzzing of wasps. He looked out to the road in front of the ministry.

Nearly two hundred middle-aged women—armed with silver spoons and plates—were chanting something and moving slowly in the direction of the Ministry of Prime-Time, a massive slab of exposed concrete. Rakesh leaned out of the arched bay window and was assailed by a trade wind's-worth of coconut hair oil; he felt faint. The woman four stories below walked like Sangita—thumping loosely from side to side, each step like a tree being uprooted, then caught in some kind of environmental debate and thrust back in just a few centimeters ahead. Mr. Ahuja placed his palms on the cool bricks and ran his fingers down the rough crevices between them. To watch a crowd eat away and corrode the city's infrastructure, to feel—even from a distance—the liters of sweat being lost for a ridiculous cause and to rise several stories above the conical boom-range of the loudspeaker, this seemed to Mr. Ahuja to be the point of living. He always wanted to be this close to mass action. He wanted to join this noncooperation movement. He wanted, for a moment, to tell these women that he—yes, *he*—would be the new Mohan Bedi, that he would negotiate the steps of the ministry and become the first man to join the Aunties, and in truth, he'd only be doing it for the crowd. Perhaps that was why TV had no appeal for him; when he was on TV giving interviews, the masses watching were abstract glitches and sparks on antennas jutting illegally from rooftops all over the country. He couldn't feel them. So he focused his vision now on the bobbed heads and the sagging banners—and that was when a face turned up at him in a flash and became Sangita. Or he thought he saw Sangita. She had been right there. He leaned farther out of the window, aware of a wasp having snipped at his neck. There, between the woman who was carrying a little boy on her shoulders and the other one who was talking on her cell phone and winding her dupatta around her fingertip even as the rest of the women screeched insults at the Ministry of Prime-Time. Would Sangita dare come out into this heat and risk a stampede when she was carrying his child? Would she actually forklift and airdrop her large self into the scene of such elbow-to-elbow action?

A thread of mango in his teeth tantalized his tongue; his fingers were striped with the pressure marks of skin against brick. He knew the answer was *no*—Sangita never even visited the vegetable market—but he felt the same unease he felt when he sat up at night with a great twitch in his left leg, the traffic outside a pulmonary roar, and remembered that Sangita could easily betray him and tell Arjun the secret whenever she wanted. At that moment his thoughts would go dense and sticky; he'd look at her half-open mouth and the expanding whorl of a polio injection on her shoulder and remind himself that she owed him everything, that in all these years he'd never sunk into true cruelty, that despite her ugliness he'd never sent her packing off to Dalhousie or confronted her parents or headed out in search of the girl he'd actually been shown on that beautiful and hopeful day in the hills months before the wedding that ruined his life.

CHAPTER 16

BRIBING AGE

At the hospital Arjun watched as Ravi called his father and explained—in quick breaths—what had happened. Arjun was secretly glad *he* hadn't been driving; he didn't want to involve his father in this. Fathers were prone to push situations to their natural extremes, undoing any reactionary restraint or compensatory aggression their sons may have learned. Ravi's father, it turned out, was in the former category: he knew no restraint. His arrival five minutes later spun a fairly controlled situation into a tizzy. He shouted at everyone. He wore glasses that skidded down his shark-fin nose. He made Ravi sit down on a chair in the tiny waiting room and scolded him to the point of tears. He asked Ravi why he didn't look when he drove. He was a tense man and he had come expecting a fight, and he was upset to find none. He couldn't handle the fact that everyone had been awfully *nice* to the boys.

For instance: when they'd arrived, the ward had been full of young women who'd slit their wrists in solidarity with Mohan Bedi, but the nurse had noted Arjun's hysteria and made extra space for the girl, ushering her into a white cuboid of fluttering curtains. The girl, too, had been relieved. She was strapped down on a stretcher, begging for painkillers. She kept talking between moans, saying again and again it was her fault—the boys were very nice, her cell phone was okay, wasn't that proof? Doctors went at her bones with flat hammers and found nothing. Tissues were damaged, mitochondria were impaired with asphyxiation, no bones were broken. Tests were summoned. Then the girl's parents—two globular specimens, slow-moving victims of diabetes and arthritis, people used to being slowly killed, out of place in the spotless clean white-lit accidental aftermath of the fancy emergency room—arrived and started dumbly text messaging their friends and family. They didn't know quite what to do with themselves; the woman's salwar swished the floor; the father stroked his chin and sagged on the side with which he carried his briefcase, telling Ravi that there was nothing to worry about. He had no interest in litigation. The girl was okay, that was what mattered. They were decent people.

Now. A smart father would have taken one look at this

propitious situation, gathered up the boys, and dashed through the exit. A smart father would have made sparkling promises to the girl's parents, gotten down on his knees, and gifted them a dud contact number. A smart father would have avoided the inevitable chitchat with the policeman who would register the accident. Failing this, a smart father would take the policeman aside and thrust a folded one-thousand-rupee note into his grubby hand. A smart father would not argue with authority.

Arjun knew because he *had* a smart father. Genetic impulses propelled him to intervene. "Uncle, the receptionist said the police-wallah is coming. It's better if we go before. Ravi doesn't have a license."

Mr. Mehta stopped scolding Ravi for a second; he pushed his gold-rimmed glasses to their summit. "The person who was *hit* is saying nothing is wrong. What is the problem?"

"Please bribe the police, Dad," Ravi implored.

"No. Nonsense," said Mr. Mehta, lifting both palms skyward in rage. "The people you hit don't want to press charges. You expect me to *bribe*? All my life I have lived in this country." He paused, rescued his glasses from tipping off his nose. "And not once have I bribed." (He was lying.) "This everything-goes attitude of yours is no good, Ravi."

Everything goes, my foot, thought Arjun. He wished Ravi would be more persuasive. *But, Dad, I don't have a license. I'll have to go to jail. I won't be able to get into college abroad. Please, Dad. These things matter to Harvard and all. Even if I have a 1500*

SAT they won't take me with a criminal record. Please, let's bribe the police-wallah.

But Ravi was gutless before his father. "Sorry, Dad. But please?"

"This is all part of growing up only," continued Mr. Mehta, wagging his index finger at Ravi. "When I was ten, my father used to send me on all sorts of errands. I had to even go to the butcher shop and buy meat—have you seen how filthy those shops are? I used to go alone to Garhi. Awful, awful place. Flies everywhere. They also expect you to bribe if you want non-fly meat. I told them go to hell. I'll eat flies. I was only ten remember. But even then I knew: better to eat flies than to feed money to people. And then I came back home with halal meat, and you know what your grandfather did? He slapped me. Slapped me straight across the face, *chaaapppatt*. Nowadays everyone wants you to be a softie. But I tell you, slaps work best. I never got bloody halal meat again—"

"But, Dad, I started driving because you wanted me to," said Ravi. "You wanted me to run errands."

"How is this relevant?"

"Sorry, Dad."

And that was that.

Arjun—nurtured on arguments, on talking back to his father—felt the full weight of Ravi's defeat as his friend balanced his head in two shaking palms. The perspective was chastening. Arjun felt bad that he'd been ornery with his own father. The regret was also convenient: Arjun needed to involve Mr. Ahuja before sanctimonious Mr. Mehta landed them in more trouble. He excused himself to make a phone call and, in doing so, missed out on a conversation between Mr. Mehta and the beat policeman that would have caused him severe palpitations.

The policeman was tapping his case register on his knee in a steady rhythm. He asked to see Ravi's license.

"I don't have it," said Ravi. "It fell down."

"How old are you?" said the policeman.

Before Ravi could lie, Mr. Mehta said, "Sixteen."

"*Sixteen?*" the policeman wheezed. "Sixteen and driving?"

"Everyone does it," said Mr. Mehta.

"Yes, yes. Everyone does it. You will have to come to the police station," he said to Ravi. "You are a minor, you are illegally driving, and you have hit someone. You have almost taken a life. Now please come. Let us go."

"You want money?" Mr. Mehta griped.

"That's not how you bribe!" said Ravi.

The policeman paced about the waiting room. He was a hassled man with two glistening velvet pouches of hair around either ear and a handkerchief with which he mopped his umbrage-taking forehead, the eyebrows pulsing upward as if to capture and harvest the sweat pouring down—and right now he was in a philosophical mood. "Whether I want money or not is irrelevant. In the long run, yes, of course, I would like money. Who doesn't like money? But, at present moment, both of my daughters are married. I do not plan to have more children except by accident. Hence I am not presently needing money. I am looking for glory. Making arrests is glory. Now, if you resist, I will be even more glorious. So, please, just come quietly. You are in the wrong. I have the law on my side."

Arjun, still on the cell phone, overhearing this last bit, turned around in horror, and said, "One second—can we wait please? A witness is coming. Please. Please. Please."

CHAPTER 17

USE THOSE CONNECTIONS

MR. AHUJA WAS IN HIS CAR—contemplating the forthcoming flattery of the SPM—when the call came.

Mr. Ahuja screamed. "WHY THE HELL WAS RAVI DRIVING?"

"Sorry, Papa. I'm in trouble—"

"DOESN'T MATTER. HOW MANY TIMES HAVE I TOLD YOU? ONLY GO IN A CAR WITH A DRIVER?"

Unlike Mr. Mehta, Mr. Ahuja's shouting was calculated—a flexing of his larynx to firmly reestablish his authority, so severely eroded by Arjun's untimely appearance in the nursery last night.

"Sorry Papa. Please come."

Then Arjun explained the complications. The dutiful policeman. Ravi's stubborn father.

"Coming," said Mr. Ahuja.

In the hospital Mr. Ahuja found the four boys crouched low over a table in the waiting room and was so relieved to see Arjun that he immediately botched the moment. "You must be the famous band," he beamed.

The boys, Arjun included, jolted upright, said their "Hello uncles."

Ravi's father looked a little upset, his cheeks twisted into a scowl.

"Where is the policeman?" asked Mr. Ahuja. "Let me talk to him."

Unnecessary. The policeman—harassing some other innocents outside the ER—simply saluted him and followed, looking pale. Mr. Ahuja was now his concentrated best, marching through the neon-lit corridors with his arms wound into his three-piece suit, his chin tucked into his neck, shoulders hunched—the entire world gets sucked in when a powerful man turns brusque and broody. He exuded importance. He had brought his two Black Cat Bodyguards—Balwant Singh and Ram Lal, former washermen—out of their laundry fellowship; they followed him with upright machine-guns. The receptionist came to meet him at the automatic doors to the waiting room, palm curled like a rose. He was so sorry. He was the one who had called the police. It was simple protocol. Now he was sorry. So, so sorry to offend the Minister-ji.

Ravi got up and kept saying thank you.

After conferring with the policeman, Mr. Ahuja said, "Okay, so we need to write out an agreement if we want to settle out of court. So—who is the driver?"

"*He* is the driver," said Arjun, a bit irritably. "I told you on the phone."

"Please be quiet. He is *not* the driver," said Mr. Ahuja, matter-of-factly. "Correct, Mr. Mehta?"

"Yes, of course."

"But we need to put a name down." Mr. Ahuja paused. "Not you boys. We need to say someone else was driving."

"How about one of your bodyguards?" said Mr. Mehta, looking askance at Balwant and Ram.

"ID card?" said Mr. Ahuja.

"Bodyguards," repeated Mr. Mehta.

"No, no," said Mr. Ahuja dismissively. "They are poor people. The last thing poor people need is their name on a legal document—"

"My driver—" said Mr. Mehta.

"No, no. If you don't mind, can you put your name?" asked Mr. Ahuja. Only it wasn't a question; it was a command. Mr. Ahuja was looking Mr. Mehta in the eye, his head tight and trembling with authority.

Mr. Mehta hesitated. "Well. There's one issue. I'm not sure—"

"Never mind," said Mr. Ahuja, appalled by Mr. Mehta's cowardice. "I will put my name down. How does it matter if I am a minister? I will say I hit the girl. I am to blame. It is my fault."

And before anyone could stop him, he'd written out a statement in Hindi and signed it. Mr. Ahuja was now officially the driver. Mr. Ahuja had hit the girl. Arjun was impressed by his father's self-sacrifice, and he understood from the lovelorn expressions on his friends' faces that they would be eternally grateful for Mr. Ahuja's intervention. That he—Arjun—could misuse their gratitude to establish complete control over the band. That he'd never have to invite them home to practice.

CHAPTER 18

A LITTLE CHAT

Mr. Ahuja did, in the end, have his revenge on Mr. Mehta. He walked into the ward, shook hands with the girl's parents, patted the girl on the head, and pointed to Mr. Mehta. "He is a great man. He has agreed to pay for all medical expenses."

Mr. Mehta frowned, assented.

"Your good name?" asked the girl's father.

"Minister Ahuja."

They signed the agreement. Then, to cement the situation, Mr. Ahuja gave the girl's parents the ultimate prize—his phone number. He told them they could call if they ever needed "help." Yes, help: in Delhi, the only thing that mattered was who you knew, and now—for the rest of their lives or for the duration of his term—the girl's parents *knew* a minister (whether they'd be able to get through Mr. Ahuja's peons and busy phones was another matter). They signed the legal document and the case was closed. Mr. Ahuja was triumphant: he inhaled deeply and took in the peculiar odor of the hospital, a smell he associated with babies being born, kick-started with a little slap on their backs to out any fluid.

He walked toward the car with Arjun. The parking lot was floodlit and finished with tiny, ugly peaks of concrete.

"Thank you, Papa."

"You're welcome, son," said Mr. Ahuja. Then he added, "I hope you're not upset about last night."

"I'm normal," said Arjun.

"It must be upsetting. What you saw last night. I'm sorry we didn't get a chance to talk about it."

"Papa, the more you ask me if I'm upset, the more upset I'll get."

Mr. Ahuja said, "Come sit here with me in the car. I need to have a father-son talk with you."

They remained standing, knees awkwardly bent in the breach between cars. Mr. Ahuja asked the driver, who had been sitting with one leg out of the car, smoking, to take a bus back home.

"I'm going to drive," he told him. The driver handed Mr. Ahuja the keys and walked away.

Mr. Ahuja gestured at the open driver's door. "Let's sit in the car and have a father-son talk."

"This *is* a father-son talk," Arjun reminded him.

"Very funny, young man. But what I am going to talk about is very serious. Get in."

"Papa, I *know* how sex works. I'm sixteen."

"No, of course, beta. Of course! In this day and age how can one not? But I also wanted to use this opportunity to talk to you about, well, a question you asked me some years ago."

"What question?"

"Well. Do you remember you asked me why your penis looks different from that of other boys?"

"What? Did I? No."

"You asked me. And I said then that it is because they have foreskin and you don't. Remember?"

"No."

There was a point to this excruciating exchange. Mr. Ahuja wanted to use Arjun's mandatory circumcision in America as a segue, applying to dialogue the same tricks of photography that showed a flower retracting into a bud in a few seconds. A concentrated life span. Circumcised penis = America = Rashmi. Later, Mr. Ahuja would wonder if this was unconscious revenge he'd taken on Arjun. Hitting back with a sexual secret.

"Please bear with me for a minute. This will all be clear to you soon. I'm not doing this to needle you. But there is a reason why they have foreskin and you don't. I want to explain it properly."

"How do you know what my penis looks like?"

"I am your father! Of course I know what every part of you looks like! I gave birth to you—"

"Mama gave birth to me," Arjun corrected. "You just watched."

"Exactly," said Rakesh, "but I washed you sometimes also."

"I don't want to talk about this."

"Okay, I understand this is a sore topic, but it is also a salient one, and I just want you to know that your penis is perfectly normal. It's different because—"

"I know! Papa, everyone can HEAR US!"

"No, no—no one can hear. We are in the parking lot."

"NO, ONLY YOU CAN'T HEAR."

"Okay, okay," said Mr. Ahuja. He decided to retreat. "I just didn't want you to think that because you are circumcised you are a Muslim or any such thing. These days there are all these movies in which people who are circumcised are mistaken for Muslims and then killed in riots or arrested as terrorists, and I just wanted you to be aware—"

"What's circumcised?"

"You know: your penis."

"I hate you," said Arjun.

"What?"

"I hate you," Arjun said, now nearly in tears. "Is this what a son needs to hear from his father? A judgment of the size of his penis? Hello, son, your penis is not regular-sized or good-sized or normal-sized, but instead, your penis is circum-sized?"

"Arjun, YOU WILL NOT RAISE YOUR VOICE AT ME!"

Arjun walked off toward the hospital gates.

Rakesh shouted behind him, "CIR-CUM-CISION MEANS YOU HAVE NO FORESKIN! IT MEANS YOU HAVE NO SKIN!"

Arjun shot back over his shoulder: "YOU HAVE NO HEART!"

The repartee hit Rakesh with the force of a tennis ball slamming into a racquet with loosened guts. His entire body vibrated around the shocked, shivering antenna of his spine. What was wrong with him? He could only keep his guilty secret by treading clumsily on his own words, each conversation with his son a disaster in the making.

The boy stood near the hospital gates with his back to him, arms crossed, hair wet and clumpy with perspiration, and now Mr. Ahuja was angry. First, Arjun's intrusion last night and now this public shouting match. He couldn't condone his son's constant disrespect. He wanted to shock Arjun into submission with the secret. This was not how he'd imagined doing it. This would not be a rehearsed and penitent explanation like talking to the villagers in his constituency about why they wouldn't have a ready supply of drinking water for another five months. This would not be a dialogue. This would not be an accidental discovery, a slipup by Sangita. This would be shouting: "THAT'S IT, ARJUN. ENOUGH IS ENOUGH. CUT IT OUT. YOU WILL NEVER SPEAK TO ME LIKE THIS AGAIN—UNDERSTAND? HOW DARE YOU RAISE YOUR VOICE AT ME. I AM YOUR FATHER AND IF YOU EVER SPEAK TO ME AGAIN LIKE THIS

THEN THAT'S IT. DON'T EXPECT HELP FROM ME, DON'T EXPECT LOVE FROM ME, DON'T EXPECT ANYTHING." Then he slipped into muttering as Arjun drew closer. "You give people love and all they do is disappoint you. I will not tolerate misbehavior from you. Understand?"

"Sorry, Papa."

"Good. Now come. Get into the car. I have something very important to tell you. Something about your mother."

But by the time Mr. Ahuja had gotten into the driver's seat and begun driving, Arjun had recouped some of his insolence. So when Mr. Ahuja said, "You know, I didn't want to marry your mother," Arjun replied, "Oh really."

Mr. Ahuja couldn't believe it. His son lacked all empathy. He'd actually raised a child who felt ruthlessly entitled. While his son scowled, Mr. Ahuja's sense of oppression on Delhi's roads was total: the hot pedals of the car jimmying tightly; the traffic around him lustrous, garish, blinding with its high beams and swarms of mosquitoes that broke upon the cars like flimsy nets; in his throat the same formulaic desiccation he felt every morning after his snack of coffee and banana; his son at his ornery worst. Then he saw himself in Arjun's eyes. A man so unapologetic in his pursuit of satisfaction that he'd camouflage his own grunts with the forced wails of his babies—but no. To expect such analysis was to expect too much. There *were* no eyes to be seen in; his son had turned away. Mr. Ahuja read his son endlessly. Arjun looked bored as he squashed a mosquito against the window. Maybe, Mr. Ahuja thought, he hadn't given Arjun enough credit. *I didn't want to marry your mother* was as self-evident as saying *I don't love her*, and Arjun knew that. (The term *your mother* too was a thorny paradox. He didn't love Sangita enough to use her real name. So he distanced her by calling her *your mother.*) Arjun had watched enough TV, in all probability, to know the ins-and-outs of arranged marriages; to know that even painstakingly matched horoscopes produced howling couples; that you could taste man and wife's indifference in the food that was served up at the table everyday. He'd seen his parents interacting every day. Now Mr. Ahuja had stated the obvious and Arjun would feel insulted rather than feel pity for Mr. Ahuja—and all Mr. Ahuja wanted was to be pitied. He wanted to be pitied for having sex with Sangita. He wanted to prove that he, too, was a victim. That he was living a life he'd had no intention of living. He couldn't stop himself.

"You don't know what your mother did to me," said Mr. Ahuja. "You have no idea. I was shown a different girl. But on the wedding day, in the tent, there was your mama. I went along because I wasn't sure. Because I didn't want to cause a fuss. Then I was sure."

Immediately, Mr. Ahuja regretted his confession. He'd sullied the memory of Rashmi with self-pity. He'd given Arjun ammunition against his siblings. He'd shown himself deeply vulnerable, capable of being cheated at life, at marriage, a man who crumbled behind his stoic façade. He was a monster battling a monster.

"Papa?" said Arjun. "Why are you telling me this?"

"Because it's true," he said.

"But that's impossible. You saw her. You married her. I don't believe it. How is this possible? It's impossible."

"She'd planned it. You're confused on your wedding night. I didn't divorce her because—"

"Confused?" Arjun sneered.

"Well—"

"Papa, she's still my mother."

"No," said Mr. Ahuja, gratefully knee-jerking, "she's not."

"What?" said Arjun. But the first thing he thought was not *I've been lied to my whole life, I've been betrayed* but *I can't believe this is the first time we've been alone together in almost a year.*

"Of course she's my real mother," Arjun shouted. "Just because you don't love her—"

"Enough!" said Mr. Ahuja. "Listen to me. What did I say before?"

"Sorry, Papa."

"Look, Arjun. This was the thing I wanted to tell you. That your Mama—Sangita—is not your real mother. Your real mother was someone else—my first wife. Look, I'm sorry I didn't tell you before. I didn't tell you because your mother died when you were three. You didn't even remember her, what was the point? I didn't want to tell you, I thought you would feel bad, I thought you'd feel different. But you're not different. You know that. Even Sangita treats you the same. Whatever she is, she's been a good mother. And I'm sorry I had to tell you like this. That's why you are circumcised—you were born in America. Most babies there are circumcised. I was doing my engineering there when you were born. We came back to India because your mother died."

"How did she die?"

"In a car accident."

"In America?"

"In America."

"Was it a love marriage?"

There was something definitive about the question; all modes of inquiry henceforth for Arjun would be sentimental—*What did she like? What did she eat? What was her favorite joke?* Even the question *Was it a love marriage?* was sentimental, but it came cloaked in an institutional reference.

"Yes," said Mr. Ahuja, "it was a love marriage."

Arjun ground his teeth and tried to look disbelieving—but failed.

Now Mr. Ahuja drove and drove and drove. They'd U-turned under the Moolchand Flyover—sped past its crumbling walls and extravagant bushes that swept the road—and had passed Defence Colony in a rash of high-beamed traffic before approaching the old 1982 Jangpura Flyover. Mr. Ahuja hadn't driven in years; it showed. His body was tense behind the steering wheel of the Qualis. Old pains resurfaced: his back ached, his shoulders ached, his arse ached, his head ached. Sitting in the back seat of his chauffeured car, he'd gotten used to making relaxed, trenchant observations about the city—now you needed to observe simply to live. Beauty be damned. He shook his fist at drivers zigzagging between lanes; he pummeled the accelerator hard to overtake a young man in a suit who'd whizzed through a red light; honked madly at a truck that had broken down in the middle of the road, its back bumper decorated with small green plants to indicate its vegetative state; and then found himself on the Jangpura Flyover, a wide concrete lung that gently breathed the car up to eye level with treetops and flocks of pigeons, his mind aware not of the aestheticism of the crossing that had once so inspired him but rather of the fact that he was crawling to the crest of the flyover. *Crawling.* This was to be the simultaneous beauty and tragedy of the flyovers: you'd escape the red lights, but the traffic was growing so fast that you'd still be jammed, your only consolation a view of Delhi from a height.

Rakesh, then, was the great consoler of Delhi. He could bandage the city with concrete, but he couldn't offer a solution to the growing number of cars or people or even the slums you levitated over in your fancy car.

And now he was getting off the Jangpura Flyover, and he was about to enter the one part of Delhi he'd not changed at all. It was too green and too beautiful and too old to change. The dry, green belt of the Yamuna Canal lying perpendicular to the road; the bulb of Humayun's tomb emerging from the tungsten-bright trees; the old Oberoi Hotel; rich colonial Delhi. He wanted to tell Arjun about his romance with Rashmi here, but how could he?

They couldn't even face each other in the car. He felt so thirsty now, the way one did after one had finally lain in bed, that thirst that arose because the body was always rolling over toward entropy, a terrible restlessness. So you got up at night, tired, and picked up a glass, took a sip. It was not a slaking sip. It was not a satisfying segue into sleep. It was just a drink to destroy that last leftover ounce of restlessness you carried back to bed.

And he felt like this was the beginning of a long sleep, this talk, this drive. A paternal hibernation. And all he wanted before this descent into alienation was a drop of encouragement from his son, one motion or sentence or word that said *Now that you've told me the secret, I will forgive you for having held it so long*. But no, that was not how it worked. For every extra year he had kept the secret, Rakesh knew he would have to pay. The words were easy enough to speak, and yes, that was what made it worse, the ease of it, the ease.

When they were driving past the huge mansions of Golf-Links Colony, Arjun asked, "Papa, do you have a photo of Mama?"

The crucial thing for Arjun was to have an image. He had caught himself thinking about how he'd dramatically confess his tragic backstory to Aarti, and was appalled by his own opportunism. He knew that if he could see a picture, any picture, he'd be cured, he'd become aware of the gravity of the situation and join his father in mourning.

Mr. Ahuja said, "Nothing. I have nothing to show."

He forgot about the tie with the cricketer pattern—that

cherished gift from Rashmi—looped lavishly around his neck. And all of Arjun's good intentions imploded again.

Rakesh had been meticulous. He had rid himself of all proof of Rashmi's existence, taking with it the self-conscious dread he had of becoming the sad widower who garlanded the portrait of his dead wife and spoke to her occasionally about what was happening in his life, how he was waiting to join her, how expensive potatoes were these days, etc. How could he explain to Arjun that this destruction was a safeguard against his own grief, not the purposeful nurturing of a secret? That he had had no choice. That he'd cupped his hands through drawers full of Rashmi's long and extravagant *To Do* lists and wept for each item that was left unchecked. Every photograph he had chucked during a trip to Manhattan into the East River. It was worth the two hundred dollars he was fined by a policeman who had caught Rakesh littering. Littering? What was wrong with this country? This country that allowed no grief? This country that fined, two hundred dollars times thirteen rupees, that is, 2600 rupees for a few photographs that had "accidentally fallen into the water due to a strong breeze, officer"?

Would the policeman have lessened his fine if he had told him the story of his suffering right then? Would his son forgive him if he understood everything?

Grief didn't seem to excuse anything. Grief was the cliché of the century. In the centuries past, men had lost wives, women had lost husbands, parents had lost children, children had lost parents. Now you couldn't bear to lose anyone.

The clothes had all been donated too—he had been too pennywise to dump them in the dustbin—and he wondered if Rashmi's saris and salwars had made their way from Goodwill to the shoulders of naïve Orientalists. If Rashmi simply lived on as a piece of exotica in each of these women's lives. As for the jewelry, he had sold it, and given the cash to Rashmi's parents in a gesture of generosity. He thought the money would calm them, but no: Rashmi's parents never forgave Rakesh for denying them their dead daughter's belongings.

What could Rakesh tell Arjun about Rashmi?

He remembered only stupid details. He remembered the way she was before Arjun was born. He remembered the superbly frigid, icicle-sharpened day in New York City when they'd taken the F train to Coney Island on a whim during their first month in America. The train's magnetic lurch propelled them toward the view as they emerged into sunlight: a giant Ferris wheel perched atop the island of magnanimous trash—a sulking, occasionally turning rotunda that seemed like it could break loose and flatten the crowds ant-hilled below. Far away, the glisten of sand meeting water. The train was nearly empty when they got off at the Aquarium stop, and all Rakesh could remember now was the fragile stem of Rashmi's wrist in his hand as he gently tugged her out of the train. She was so absentminded. She never knew where to get off. She liked to sit and watch, never afraid to make eye contact with the strangers across from her because, well, she was probably seeing right through them. Yet sometimes she noticed things that even Rakesh's IIT-honed brain didn't observe. Such as:

the Ferris wheel had two layers of bogies, like a gear with teeth on both sides. Unlike in India.

I'm afraid of giant wheels, she said.

We don't have to go, said Rakesh.

No let's.

Why?

They went. It was only on top that she answered his question and told him the story. She wasn't afraid of giant wheels; she was terrified. When she was four, her parents put her in the rickety carriage of a giant wheel at a Diwali fair in Delhi along with her six-year-old cousin, Amit. The giant wheel was manually operated—two emaciated yet muscular men dressed strictly in dhotis climbed up and down the metallic bars of the wheel to keep the mechanism in rotation—and you could feel the hotness of their breaths as they passed by your compartment, their simian feet clenched tight on metal. The whoosh you felt in your stomach was doubled because of the voyeuristic thrill of wondering: *Will these men fall and die? What if they fall?* But it wasn't a real concern, because weren't you paying them for exactly that? To have these poor men take mortal risks so that you could feel a little frightened for your life as you swung fifty feet above the ground?

Rashmi, poor darling four-year-old Rashmi had huddled with her cousin in the creaky cradle, heard the other children whooping with joy, felt her hands whitening around the protective metal bar, wondered if this is what it felt like to be a bird on a branch in a storm, and did the only thing she could:

she screamed. Rashmi's scream was the longest scream anyone on the giant wheel had ever heard. Unlike most screams that started and ended, Rashmi's scream bloomed to a crescendo as if she was trying to blow a balloon. With nothing but fear. Minutes passed. One of the giant wheel operators almost fell off, and Amit was so ashamed of his four-year-old cousin that he nearly leaped from the trolley. Eventually, a particularly confident operator climbed up to her trolley, grabbed her from the perch, and carried her down all the way.

Down the rolling staircase of metal bars. Down the sickening roll of the wheel. Down with and against gravity.

It was the most scared I've ever been, Rashmi said. You'd think climbing up something is scarier, but climbing down through a jungle of metal with some strange man holding you in one hand and holding on for dear life with the other—I stopped screaming and just held my breath. When I got down it was like I had just taken a dive in a really deep pool and then gotten out after holding my breath for ten minutes.

Why in the world are we on this thing right now? Rakesh asked.

Why? she said.

Yes, why.

That's easy, she said. I wanted to remember why I was screaming.

The scream came to him through layer after layer of time; the grief of losing Rashmi was the grief of having forgotten all the stories she was yet to tell him. The pain of telling Arjun about Rashmi would be that she could never be explained into existence.

"Does anybody else know about this?" Arjun asked.

He wanted to know if his betrayal was complete. He understood why his father had confessed to him while driving—you can't get out of a moving car.

"Obviously, your Mama—I mean, Sangita—knows."

The horizon was a dashboard, and his mind needled through the years with the mathematical energy of the speedometer. Only Mama knew. His betrayal was only one-thirteenth complete. Or two-fourteenth. Or one-seventh. He grew irritated. A brain, like a speedometer, never shut off; it quivered endlessly near 0.1.

"What about Varun, Rishi, Rita—"

"Yes, I told them today. I told them they must never ever treat you differently, and that if they did, I would give them hell."

"Wonderful. So that's how they're going to love me more?" asked Arjun. "As a stepbrother?"

"No, beta. Half-brother."

"I don't want to live here anymore," he said dramatically. "I want to go to America."

"Beta—"

"No, I want to go," said Arjun.

"Beta, you have never even been there. You don't even know how it is, do you? This is just a childish insistence. Life there is very hard—no servants, no family, no social life—you're always an outsider, you want that?"

"Papa—"

"And, besides, you have always told me that in Class 12, America will be a backup only, so why do you want to go there now? Is it because you were born there? Firstly, you are not a citizen anymore and you don't have a visa and visa is hard enough to procure." Rakesh had made sure to decline Arjun's American citizenship as part of his elaborate coverup of Rashmi's existence. "And, beta, what do you think you will feel when you go back? You have no memory of how it was, so what will you gain? And what will you remember? That your—"

"Papa—"

"That your Mama died there?" said Mr. Ahuja. "Listen to me right now. There is nothing in America that there is not here. Don't think you can just leave all the people you love and go away somewhere else. You can go once you're old enough to take care of yourself, but you're not right now and that's all."

"I'm old enough. I'm almost as old as everyone else who goes."

"Beta, that's not it, you are not grasping my point! Look at me. I returned, right? I saw America and I saw India, and I came back and decided to help the people and how sad will it be if my own children are leaving this country? What's the point of trying to make this country a better place if all the smart people leave?"

"But you didn't come back for India. You said you came back because your wife died."

CHAPTER 19

DRIVEWAY DECISIONS

When they arrived home, Arjun ended their mutual brooding with a loud clang of the passenger door and jogged off toward the house. Mr. Ahuja let it pass. The car was comfortable, its headlights fixating on the cracks in the driveway, the nocturnal chains of ants heave-hoing over hillocks of moss. Mr. Ahuja adjusted his tired eyes to the squat off-white colonial house and his soaked collar to the rapidly-evolving tropical weather in the car. What a screw-up. He was a fool to have waited so long to tell Arjun. To have waited till the point where his son had mastered the means, the vocabulary, to hurt him back. Waited till the brink of his son's independence, offering this news like a parting shot.

But he had to be objective about himself: He *had been* so bloody tortured. How exactly would he have told him? And hadn't he assumed that the year-by-year erosion of memory would help him get over Rashmi—make it easier for him to spill the secret? But he hadn't gotten over Rashmi one bit, and how could he? How could he if he'd married a woman like Sangita?

It was an awful thing to admit, but he was plain ashamed to be seen with Sangita. Marrying her was charity enough. For a man who was a champion of form—a man who shivered like a newborn baby when you whisked him down a flyover, a golfer who'd once spent ten minutes on his knees on a golf course just patting up the evenness of the grass, a spectator who marveled year after year at the symmetry of soldiers during the Republic Day parade, a man for whom form was *religion*—he'd gotten stuck with the least elegant woman possible. Still his mind soldiered on. His body and brain collaborated to ignore her formlessness. Even then, he couldn't forget Rashmi: when they weren't having sex, Sangita was the very manifestation of his betrayal—in remarriage, in life. Together they lived in a giant house where the lights were constantly blowing their fuses, and you stood in silence with one hand on a light switch while above the bulb burst into sublunary flames. Then vanished. She was the element of dark irony in his life. She made God's revenge on him—one dead wife, one switched wife—comical. And now, after Arjun's intrusion, even the possibility of sex had dried up.

Recoiling from the image, Mr. Ahuja grasped the steering

wheel, inhaled the dead-animal musk of the car, ventilated his senses. Sangita's face thus forgotten, there remained an overpowering notion in the anterior chamber of his nose. Entering the brain. The understanding that if he ever wanted to have sex again, it would have to be outside the house. The house was the problem, not sex.

He was parked in his own driveway. He could back out at will. He could follow the overhead power lines to a home spasming with light. He'd have an affair. He'd have many affairs. He was one of the most powerful men in Delhi. So what if he was only attracted to pregnant women. He could change, disengage from his fantasies. Or if not change, then arrive at a compromise: proposition bloated women who felt unloved, misshapen, fart-ready. Remind them that it was safe for them, too, to have affairs. That the sex was never better, and they couldn't get pregnant if they were already pregnant.

But what if he was only attracted to women who carried *his* children? What would he do then? Divorce Sangita? Remarry? Find a younger girl? Repeat the cycle? Father fifty-five children? Father a nation?

Rakesh Ahuja! You fool!

The case thus closed, he loosened his grip on the gearshift and pondered more practical matters.

How would the children respond if Arjun attacked them with this information about the bride-switch? Would they stick to Mr. Ahuja's instructions, not ostracize him? And Sangita, what would she think? He wished now that his children didn't have to witness what would transpire with Arjun; he wished, in fact, that they were all unborn, and his thoughts turned on the baby that was due in September. He focused all his hopes on that child. He'd get that one right. The baby was still a precious lump in Sangita's stomach, but it would eventually be born, and in its ferocious struggle to escape the womb, Rakesh would witness a celebration of his own power, his howling love for life, his lust, his virility—yet, the baby, when it finally woke to the world and came of age, would know him, Mr. Ahuja, only in the twilight of his life.

If only he could speak to the child now. If only he could tell the child his dreams and fears and ambitions. If only he could lay his head on that smooth surface and whisper . . .

With a jerk of the hand brake, Mr. Ahuja—lacking both a sturdy alibi and a secret lover—backed the car out of the driveway and drove to the SPM's residence.

CHAPTER 20

HELLO, AARTI

Of course, Arjun didn't want to go to America: America, like Rashmi, was beside the point. He just wanted to feel special again—to feel loved and admired by his Papa for reasons that were sewn into the fabric of his personality—as opposed to being jerked around on the end of a bungee cord thrown from a point in the past that was unreachable. He wanted to plummet back into familiar patterns immediately. Play out his daily routine to its limit. Go switcheroo a baby's diaper, gasp at the audacious stylings of Mama's knittings, bully the hell out of his siblings. Not that he thought of it as bullying, but what else was the correct term for accusing Sahil of being a girl, and then challenging a scared five-year-old to an arm-wrestling showdown? The act of bullying was a sacred one, like the occasional flooding of dry land, a message that one's life was always lived in the shadow of chaos and uncontrollable forces—that if you were a three-year-old and felt jealous of the newborn and attempted to chuck an ashtray at it, a whole year's worth of correction would await you, you'd find yourself at a table with all the seats taken, you'd go out in the playground and suddenly be paying obeisance to a large puddle of mud, you'd go on a car trip and remain locked in with the windows up because only dogs died in hot cars—not humans. Bullying, then, was a reminder you were human. It was a reminder you were related.

But today his purpose was very much the opposite. He wished to taunt his siblings till they broke down and said: *Whatever, you're just a stepbrother.* Till they said: *Fuck you, we owe you nothing*. Till they said: *You're an untouchable in our eyes.*

Or something dramatic like that.

Unfortunately, there were no experimental subjects to be found. Rita and Tanya's room was empty—they were probably helping Mama unclip the laundry from the sagging clotheslines in the garden. Rishi was sitting on a stool in the lobby folding a paper plane from a stiff, crackling copy of the *Times of India*; Arjun felt simultaneously too grandiose in his needs to bother with such an easy victim and also secretly afraid of the damaging effects of Rishi's signature "sorry flurries" on his spongy psyche.

• • •

Finding no one to bully, Arjun decided to, ahem, bully himself: He retired to the bathroom to masturbate. First, he was gentle. He very nonviolently examined his circumcised penis. He wanted to find images of similar penises on the Internet, but that is something a man cannot do: Google his own penis. So he tried to masturbate to a vision of Aarti. The attempt ended in failure and chafing. This meant that he *must really like Aarti*, he decided. When he liked (as in *really liked*) a girl, he couldn't bring himself to think about touching her, holding her, penetrating her. He could only think about marrying her. Besides, he had inherited from his mother a love for the classified section of the newspaper; he scanned it now and read the marriage section of the *Times of India* with the varying empathies of a suitor, a bridegroom, a dowry-less girl, and a horny student.

Marriage. Yes. He tried to imagine having sex with Aarti in a wedding tent, their legs double-helixed, a garden full of sexy special-effect dust, crowds of people picking their noses. But he couldn't *hear* the crowds. The house was bizarrely and insultingly quiet. The tap next to the toilet was dripping into a blue plastic mug. Rishi knocked on the door and said, "Scuba diving or what?"

Arjun toppled the mug and exited sheepishly. "I left fish for you in the toilet," he said to Rishi.

He figured he'd just have to try masturbating again later. Or would that be futile.

He needed a strong glass of scotch in order to decide. He

went to the dining room and stood romantically before the liquor cabinet. His father never drank. He himself—a rock star!—had never drunk. The cabinet was locked; it taunted him with a great rattle of the shelf when he tugged on the knob; he gave up. He stared at the reflection of his face as it was distorted between the columns and columns of brown liquor, their labels removed in the interests of democratic drinking—a giant refraction chamber. To resemble someone or something you've never seen was to be diminished, boxed, predetermined. What did his real Mama look like? Was she simply all that was left when you subtracted from Arjun's face all of Papa's features? Take away the unruly eyebrows. Lop off the hooked nose. Sandpaper away the first grain of stubble. What was she now? What? A human pear. A rotten, fetid human pear with eyes. An ugly piece of modern art. An abstraction. A nothing. She was the true stepmother, a veiled tyrant ushered into his life nearly two decades after he'd been born.

In the nursery Mrs. Ahuja was readying to throw herself—body, knitting, buttocks, and all—on a chair. Free fall at 9.8 meters per second squared was her idea of sitting, and the fate of the plastic dark glasses on the chair was a straightforward flattening.

He said, "Watch out, Mama."

The house had been littered with dark glasses ever since the last conjunctivitis scare; for five days the children had all worn shades and walked about the house with a funereal solemnity. Papa's old briefcases appeared out of nowhere. Sahil, six, was seen moping over a sheaf of paper. Soon, however, it was determined that the conjunctivitis scare was just that: a scare.

Mrs. Ahuja sat on the shades after all.

Arjun held the arms of the white plastic chair, wincing, bemoaning. But it was routine wincing, bemoaning and so he enjoyed it. "Mama, you should wait. I was telling you—"

"If you had said: Wait, wait, wait, then I would understand. And how come you are not looking? Babies are doing the latrine—"

Still she made no effort to retrieve the crushed plastic.

"Mama—"

"Accha. Where is he? Kindly tell him to come here, and—"

Arjun had a 97.6 percent success rate in ascertaining who exactly Sangita's ephemeral "he" referred to; today he rightly assumed it was—

"Shankar!" he shouted. "Shankar!"

Shankar arrived, pulling at his Hitler mustache like it was a rotten Band-Aid. He had an empty tray in his hand.

"Bring the broom," Sangita commanded. "Then put two stools on top of each other, stand on them, and then kill the mosquitoes on the roof. Obviously, switch off fan first. Otherwise you will get a free haircut? You are seeing? Then bring bucket. Fill with water. Then tell bachas to come inside. Then throw on verandah. Understand? Understand? How dirty it is now. Dirty, dirty."

At leisure, Shankar took off one of his rubber Hawaii chappals, kneeled, and held it up as if to squash an insect. Of course there was no insect. Only Mrs. Ahuja throwing the broken dark glasses on the ground.

"What are you doing? Take this," she said, kicking the glasses. "Go take this. Tell her she can give it to him."

"Mama! At least use the maid's name," said Arjun. "Shanti. She's been here one year. And don't give the broken glasses to her."

"One tho I am doing the charitable act and you are saying this," she said in English. "In front of servant that also!"

"He understands English—" Arjun hissed, pointing to Shankar.

Shankar played dumb. Mrs. Ahuja played dumb. All the babies begged for milk.

"Sleep!" said Mrs. Ahuja. It was her one stock phrase. "Babies! Sleep!"

Arjun went one-by-one from baby Vikram to baby Gita to baby Sonali and crossed their tiny arms and legs like they were baby yogis doing baby yoga. He loved making toddlers perform their little exercises. They appeared to love it too. They gurgled and spat. Then Arjun said, "Mama. What happened to Rohan Trivedi?"

Shankar had just left. He'd forgotten his slipper on the floor. Mrs. Ahuja kicked it away and said, "Rohan Trivedi? Who is Rohan Trivedi?"

"Your TV star who died, nah. You only told me about him. I saw many women on the street today. They were doing all sorts of chanting-shanting. On Mathura Road there was a big traffic jam—that is why I was late today."

"Where are you getting this misinformation. His name is Mohan Bedi."

Arjun was stunned. "I'm becoming like Papa."

"He is dead only," proclaimed Mrs. Ahuja grimly.

"He's not coming back?"

"How can he come back? He died. Cell-o-phone was in tub."

Arjun considered this. "Mama, you should have done a protest. Now he is dead. What will happen to his wife? Have you even thought about her?"

"She is having a boyfriend. Boyfriend will become husband, nah."

This was a revelation for Arjun: that women on Indian TV had boyfriends.

"Mama," he said, teasing, "did you ever have a boyfriend?"

"Boyfriend? Are you not seeing I am married? So many children I am having."

"But when you were younger. Before you were married. People in your time had boyfriends also."

"Of course. That is what I am saying only. I had one boyfriend also."

"Really? What was his name?"

She gulped. "Chintoo."

"Chintoo! What a goonda name! How did he become your boyfriend?"

"This much I don't remember. I am an old lady. I am having a baby. How you expect me to remember?"

Arjun laughed. "Why didn't you marry *him* only?"

"I was from rich family. He was from poor family. He was the gardener's son." She continued. "When I was little, I thought marriage was a thing between brother and sister. Why? Because my Mummy called my Papa 'brother' or 'brother-what-are-you-saying.'

"Of course, I didn't know any married people. 'What is this shaadi business?' I asked my mother. She said, 'It is what we did to have you.' As you are imagining, this was zero help.

"Then one day I was sitting, and this boy Chintoo came and said, 'Will you marry me.' I said, 'Okay.'

"Later, I felt very bad, of course. Because how was I to tell him that we could not get married if we were not brother and sister? So I said to my Mummy, please adopt Chintoo. She said no. End of story."

"Classic. Classic story," Arjun said, laughing. "But how did you and Papa get married?"

"Are you not remembering? Arranged."

He remembered all right. The story the children had been told was this: Mama had once been beautiful. Papa had seen her and been smitten. Children were idiots and believed anything.

"I know! But how?"

"She said why don't you marry him, and then he said maybe you should and I said yes."

"Accha? I thought it was different. Papa told me that you tricked him!"

He tried to say this as lightly as possible—to present it as a joke—and he had hoped his tone of voice would convey to Sangita a crucial message: that he knew everything but still loved her. That he was willing to dismiss Papa's ridiculous claims.

"Eh?"

"Papa told me that you tricked him! That he was shown another girl and then you showed up!"

Mrs. Ahuja's expression had hardened this time. She pursed her lips and smiled with great effort at the hive of knitted wool she'd picked up. It didn't work. She simply looked tired and hurt; she slumped in her chair and examined her swollen feet; she refused to smile back at him.

"Yes, yes. That is what happened only," she mumbled. "Your Papa was tricked. But I was tricked also."

"I'm joking, Mama!"

But she remained unmoved.

"I'm sorry, Mama," said Arjun. "I was joking only. Papa was telling me a joke. I love you."

"What is this love-shove business," said Mrs. Ahuja. "You think I cannot joke? I was joking also." Then she segued. "Mohan Bedi was good man. Now he is dead. End of story." Then another segue. "Babies are crying. Tell Rita and Tanya to come. Babies need milk."

Tell Rita and Tanya to come. No command could have been more hurtful to Arjun at that moment. There he was, standing at her command, a fully operational baby-watching machine, and she'd asked for younger replacements. Now there was nothing for Arjun to do but despise himself. He was a stepson. Whatever affections he'd garnered from Sangita, he was going to lose for good, he knew it. Mama, Papa, Rashmi: all gone, squandered. Papa lost when Arjun uttered his cruel remark—*You came back because your wife died*—and banged the car door shut. His siblings ganging up on him and calling him *an untouchable stepbrother*, misunderstanding. An uprising of the underlings. Him being booed at the concert. He was awful and alone.

His mistake had been to rely on crowds. Crowds could turn against you.

Take the band: What if Ravi's father confiscated his drums? What if Ravi was slapped and slapped till he quit the band? He'd been foolish to imagine that Mr. Ahuja's authority in the hospital could outdo the authority of Ravi's father in his own house. Ravi was probably being scolded right this second for his accident.

Which meant: he'd have to win Aarti on his own.

He switched on the computer in the hallway and logged into Hotmail.

From: Arjun Ahuja <badfan1991@hotmail.com>

To: Aarti Gupta <aar2d2@yahoo.com>

Date: April 20

Subject: Stuff

Dear Aarti,

How r u??? sorry 2 b emailing so la8. Just wanted to say: I like you a lot. A lot. Plz don't feel weird n all bout this. Jus being honest. Also,

I made this 4 u.

```
 **        **            ** **                    **                         **   **
/**       /**           /** /**                  ****                       /**  //
/**       /**  *****    /** /**  ******         **//**    ******   ****** ****** **
/********** **///**   /** /** **////**       **  //**  //////** //**//*///**/ /**
/**//////**/*******   /** /**/**   /**      **********  *******  /** /   /** /**
/**      /**/**////    /** /**/**   /** **  /**//////** **////**  /**     /** /**
/**      /**//******  *** ***//****** //*  /**     /**//********/***     //** /**
//       //  //////  /// ///  //////   /   //      //  //////// ///       //  //
```

[Actually he hadn't "made it"; he hadn't sat still for hours carefully dropping asterisks over the imaginary stencil of her name. He'd simply patronized one of the many ASCII-generating Web sites.]

Btw—in case ure wunderin, thatz a comma after

Hello.

Gnite!!!!

Arjun

With that e-mail Arjun felt as if his life's work had been completed. He'd exposed himself. He'd finally braved humiliation. Immediately he was devastated. The spasms of hunger in his stomach came quicker and quicker. He realized he hadn't eaten dinner: dinner, like lunch, was delayed. And he'd made a mistake. He'd stupidly stated the obvious: I like you. Fool! Idiot! There was a twitching in his back, like the awkward flexing of nubs left by torn wings. He'd be needled endlessly if his friends found out. Even if they didn't, how would he possibly face Aarti now? What if she never replied to his e-mail? Worse: What if she replied-ALL to her entire school? What if not another word was spoken about this? Did she even like him? What was there to like? His hair combed in a floppy center part? The pants that tickled at his ankles? His affected swagger that friends often said looked like that of a drunken man about to topple over? Wasn't that a compliment though? How many people of his age were drunk and about to topple over?

Also: Why had he been sent to an all-boys' school? Didn't people realize that it produced men capable only of copulation not conversation?

He wrote her another e-mail.

From: Arjun Ahuja <badfan1991@hotmail.com>

To: Aarti Gupta <aar2d2@yahoo.com>

Date: April 20

Subject: Stuff

Dear Aarti,

Sorry about the last email. I dint send it—my friends are here and playing a joke. I am sorry.

Arjun

Post-e-mail-#2, it took him exactly five seconds to realize he'd made another mistake. Why would the friends needle him about Aarti unless he'd told them he liked her? Crap. Now he'd sent her not one but two self-incriminating e-mails. Oh well.

Hello, Aarti.

CHAPTER 21

MEET THE NEW PRIME MINISTER

RAKESH WAS WELL KNOWN IN THESE PARTS: he chattered informally with the liveried staff and walked straight into the SPM's drawing room. In the space of a day, 7 Ram Ram Marg had been converted from a bustling fishmarket of flattery, a place where adoring followers actually camped out in the garden for days on end in makeshift tarpaulin tents to gain the SPM's audience—had gone from being like the court of Louis the XIV to a brilliantly lit ashram. A sanctuary. A meditation chamber. A place where bare feet pattered in soft steps on the soft carpet—Rakesh looked down. He was nearly *creeping*. He was beside himself with suspense. He wondered if he was too late to rekindle his ties with the

SPM. He'd been too wrapped up in personal problems to pursue a full inquiry into the matter.

An answer awaited him in the drawing room. There he found a mirror image of his own conference with the SPM earlier that morning: a young man crossing his pajama'd legs in stiff but confident posture as the SPM regaled him with some trademark story. Four bowls of snacks laid out on the table. The napkins in the napkin holder still blowing in the fan blast. Rakesh knew immediately who the man was and what was happening. Yes. The man—wearing one of those minimalist designer kurtas, stark white with an intricate necklace of embroidery around the collar, face fashionably charcoal-sketched with stubble—was Mohan Bedi; it had to be. He was in his mid-twenties at the most. A cherub with pink lips despite the gangsterish disposition. Cheeks baggy with having been pulled too much by cooing aunties. On seeing Mr. Ahuja, the supposed-Mohan shifted into a more aggressively male position: legs spread wide, hands sternly clasped near his chest, his torso neatly reclining. Maybe he was simply avoiding the SPM's force-feeding. Her fingers indicated the four snack bowls constantly in hypnotic circles. She had changed out of the morning's saffron sari into white widow's garb.

She was probably begging him back to TV life. For the sake of the party. For the sake of the country. To placate her unforgiving party of resigners.

On seeing Rakesh, Rupa stood up with much effort and flashed a mischievous grin. "Ah. Ahuja. Perfect timing. How are you?"

Rakesh bent down, touched her feet, and sprang back up.

"Fine, ji. And you? Looking lovely as ever. Thank you for seeing me. All I need is your blessings."

"No," she said, "thank you for coming."

Then, turning to Mohan Bedi and looking askance at Rakesh, she said, "Meet the new Prime Minister."

Because his hearing was strained, and the SPM's gesture at this late hour was loose, vague, a twirl of the wrist come unstuck from its associated muzzle of words, and moreover the man who woud be Mohan Bedi had leaped out of his chair to touch his feet, Mr. Ahuja thought, not unfairly, that *he* was being introduced as the new PM. Even if the statement was a joke, he assumed *he* was it's handsome subject.

After all, the SPM knew the embattled post of Prime Minister was often on Rakesh's mind. While most governments in the past decade had nominated a puppet Prime Minister—an elected head of state that deferred to an unaccountable behind-the-scenes Rupa Bhalla–style lynchpin—the KJSZP(H202) Party had done away entirely with the pretense. For the first time in history, India hadn't had a Prime Minister. The country itself was strangely sedate on the issue, the stock market whistled its ebullient electronic tune, the sun still blasted away at the earth and its inhabitants with irritating effulgence, men and women still risked beatings and violence to cast their votes—only party members had protested. It became a hot-button issue. The post of PM was a crucial one, they argued, and it would help diffuse power, wouldn't it? What did Madam think? Madam thought nothing. Madam said nothing. Simply sat on a throne and smiled her threatening fixed smile, all her teeth jagged like the peaks of crushed glass adorning the top of unscalable walls.

So the party members—Rakesh included—tried bribing her with the idea that having a PM would, in fact, concentrate power in her *favor.* She could pick her second-in-command for the world to see, present him as her most trusted public aide, privately crush his spirit, and continue on with the glorious mission of being an autocrat in a democracy.

To this idea she seemed receptive. She kept saying she was choosing a PM, just give her time. Rakesh knew he was one of the finalists for this fantasy job. But he'd assumed he'd drastically damaged his chances—first with his unpopular stance on the Muslim issue, then with his feisty resignation letter, and finally with his opportunistic scheming. Unless: she respected the forthrightness of his resignation. Or: if she hadn't read it at all. And: Hadn't heard about his magnificent lying at the Meeting of Pay Scales. Why else would she offer him this post if not for his unwavering support?

Mohan Bedi had vacated his seat and was touching Mr. Ajuha's feet in a show of respect. He ruffled the supine boy's hair the way one pets a dog. Mohan Bedi, lifting himself up from his haunches with a flap of the arms, perfumed the room with the cologne secreted in his armpits. Mr. Ahuja was overwhelmed. His luck had finally turned. He didn't need to apologize for the letter.

"What is this PM business?" he said gruffly, gladly, to the SPM. "This is unexpected."

"Yes, it was, Uncle," said Mohan Bedi, "that is why I want your blessing."

Uncle. That word was like a Q-tip shoved straight past the terrible stalactites of wax in his ears and into the troubled brain, where it turned and turned and turned, shoveling out gray matter. Uncle. I am your uncle, you are my prime minister: No! He had walked into a terrible joke. This TV star who spoke like an awestruck child simply could not be the Prime Minister. Comedy was comedy, but this was otherworldly grotesque.

"Your good name?" said Mr. Ahuja, for the sake of severity.

"Prakash Singh."

"Not Mr. Mohan Bedi?"

"No, Uncle! Mohan Bedi is my screen name, Uncle. My real name is Prakash."

"You look thunderstruck, Ahuja!" said Rupa, slapping her knee. "Here, I will order namkeen lassi. Two times a day is good for you."

"No thank you, ji," said Rakesh. He patted his stomach to divert attention from his admittedly fallen face. His muscles worked overtime to keep the mask of earnestness in place.

The SPM started again. "You know I don't like being refused on the issue of lassis. And that is hardly a paunch worthy of a man as powerful as—"

"Rupa-ji. Is this a joke?" Rakesh interrupted. "Don't mind," he said, turning to Mohan, "but is this a joke?"

"No, Uncle," the boy stuttered. "No, Uncle."

Rupa sighed. "But I can see why you feel this way. Of course, I can see! Very easy to understand actually. You are thinking, What experience does this young boy have—" She patted him on the back. "Well, it is not experience that is important. But bravery! Courage! Strength! This bright young man over here wanted to leave the show. So he did. At the height of his popularity. What courage. But, as you know, all of the people in this party wanted him back so badly—didn't they, Mohan?—that I thought, okay, they can have him back. As their leader!"

She cackled. So there it was, thought Rakesh. She'd had her revenge on the resigning hordes by giving them what they wanted *par excellence*. And she'd had her revenge on him, Rakesh, by denying him the post he had so truly deserved, the job he'd had in mind when he'd made his ministerial reputation with the flyovers. She had won. This was why she was the Super Prime Minister and he was not.

"But I don't understand," said Rakesh. "He is not a Member of Parliament—"

"Yes, yes." Rupa yawned. "That also, bhaiya, I have taken care of. Why are you worrying? Late Satish Kumar's seat is now available. As a result, there is a by-election in his district in Bihar one week from now. The Rajya Sabha seat. From there he will run."

Mohan added congenially, as if to erase doubt, "I have had an interest in politics since young age, Uncle. My late father was a magistrate in U.P. My mother was active in village panchayats. All my chachas and taujis, they were IAS officers.

I know men in every place. I have a man in the tax department. I know the heads of all corporations through advertising campaigns. Sanyo. BPL. Videocon. Reliance. Airtel. All CEOs are my friends. With some of them I have even played golf. These connections, obviously, I would like to use to whatever ends possible."

"Very impressive," said Mr. Ahuja sarcastically. Then he turned to Rupa. "Maybe you can get me a job being the new Mohan Bedi?"

But this elicited no response from Rupa. Her right hand twitched nervously as she stared blankly at the paintings on the wall. She seemed to be not listening. He had never seen her like this, this serious. And that was when Rakesh understood: he was right, this was too comic even for Indian politics. Even the comedian-in-chief, the SPM, knew it.

This was tragedy masquerading as comedy. Appointing a guileless TV star as the Prime Minister was the rhetorical move of a person at the very end of her tether. Rupa Bhalla had realized that she was isolated in the party, and instead of resigning, she'd chosen to implode in a great fit of ridiculousness. Rakesh understood; he had done the same by marrying Sangita. The only difference between him and Rupa was that Rupa Bhalla had no regrets. He'd never known her to doubt herself. She wouldn't be calling everyone up and saying she was sorry for picking Mohan Bedi as her deputy, whereas Mr. Ahuja exploded and then whimpered his sorries. He was not fit to take revenge. He was always reneging.

He had come, he remembered, to apologize about his letter.

"What about my letter?" he asked. "What did you think? Are you suspending Yograj?"

"Ah, yes," she said. "The famous letter you sent me, how could I forget, baba? You know what my first thoughts were when I read it after you left? That I should have it framed. But you also, Ahuja, you are always throwing spanners in my works. How can I get it framed if you sent it via the e-mail? Tell me? See, that is the problem. When paper is there, I remember. When e-mail is there, I forget. E-mail I cannot frame."

"Yes, ji. And?"

"I have forwarded your e-mail to all your resigned colleagues for their consideration. I hope you are happy? Haan-ji?"

"Thank you, Rupa-ji," said Rakesh. "I shall now be going."

He had better be going. He could feel his left eyeball rattling in its cage of nerves. As he walked out, he placed both hands on his eyes and tried to convince himself that it was his sinuses. That he wasn't plain uneasy. That the sadness he felt for Rupa's imminent departure—the automatic sadness one feels when a towering personality, howsoever evil, is about to be toppled; the realization that life hereon for them will be a crushing chore of humiliation—wasn't preemptive sadness for himself. After all, he'd lost Rupa's patronage—lost Rupa altogether—and his resignation letter, that scribbled stupidity, was doing the rounds of the party's upper echelons. Exposing his utter contempt for the Hindu nationalist engine that powered his peers.

These could be his last days in the KJSZP(H202), the party that had been his life.

Mr. Ahuja drove home. Delhi appeared to be cleansed, dipped in Dettol and covered in yellow pointy neem leaves. It must have drizzled when he was in the SPM's drawing room because the mascara of smog ran dark in drains, the air so clean that Mr. Ahuja didn't blink for a full minute and scarcely noticed it. From his car window Delhi seemed as solid and surreal as the inside of a paperweight: not a beggar in sight under the Secretariat Flyover, the gardener at the entrance to his house holding down the mouth of his hose pipe so that water peacocked out across the shrubbery, his free hand saluting Mr. Ahuja who realized that he, too, lived in a bubble, in Central Delhi, Manicured Delhi, Delhi of Roundabouts, Cluster of Bureaucratic Juggernauts. The clutch was tight so he pressed down. His thigh muscles were swimming in lactic acid. He was sweaty, tired, grubby; he was home.

The forbidding iron-and-bamboo gate to his house was decorated with twisted tin plates that had been painstakingly calligraphed in fluorescent greens and bright reds by his children. These plaques issued dire warnings before disappearing from view as the guard swung back the gates:

TRESSPASSERS WILL BE PROSECUTED

BEWARE OF GARD

PRIVAT PROPERTY

LINGER HERE / BE SHOT LIKE DEER

WELCOME TO AJUHA HOUSE, POPULATION 21

The signs lightened his mood as he parked the car. He hadn't corrected their silly mistakes; mistakes were exactly what one cherished sometimes about one's children.

The house, too, he'd refused to renovate. The great colonial bungalow before him twinkled on its private sea of grass. He loved it as it was—its powdery white walls, expansive rooms, the high ceilings that overlooked a circus of convection currents, the ancient wire-insulating wooden tubes running at sharp angles along the walls before imploding in the round black plastic terminals of this or that light switch—and all of a sudden, entering through the front door, he was sad he'd spent so little time here with his children. They surrounded him immediately, and he wanted to hug them and kiss them, and so he did. He noticed everything about them: the gluey smell of their bodies; their sickly thin limbs; the girls with their braids they'd inherited from Sangita (braids that were easily pulled and thus led to frequent fights); the boys wearing sleeveless basketball shirts with American brands printed in absurd fonts; the varied fuzziness of their cheeks as he went around twisting them to unlock the steel smiles of their braces.

Only Arjun was missing. He was sitting at the dinner table with his feet kicking at one of its solid legs. The rest of the children joined him in their regular dinner positions. Mr. Ahuja at the head; Sangita at the other end; Arjun only an elbow away from his father.

It was a solemn meal. Mr. Ahuja tried to concentrate on the mechanics of eating—the rippled plain of daal across his plate, the symmetrical mounds of aalu and gobi he lined up before blasting them away with powerful scoops of his chappati, the dollops of yogurt he used to neutralize the burned spices—but it didn't work. He ate indiscriminately and rapidly and in semi-panic. He was aware of Arjun's actions on the next chair: his slow, sulking marionetted movements. As for the other children, he couldn't gauge any change in their behavior. Nor in Sangita's. Apparently there hadn't yet been a massive confrontation between Arjun and his siblings and stepmother. She in particular was as placid and contented as ever. She was eating massive quantities of daal. Mr. Ahuja remembered how, early in the marriage, he'd tried to send her on a slimming diet and had failed. Later, he'd brought up the issue in a highly erotic moment: *Darling, yes, I feel so good, I like to get you pregnant because then at least you are eating so much for a good cause!*

Good cause, indeed! Thirteen bloody good causes!

"I have news for all of you," he said.

"What, Papa?"

"I have resigned."

The children's jaws hung low with gobs of daal. In musical progression, hands fell on quivering laps. This was exactly the effect he'd intended to generate. Only Tanya had the courage to ask, "Why, Papa?"

Mr. Ahuja sat back in his chair and stared at the whirling fan above him; his body snapped instinctively into his favored posture for gravitas—shoulders relaxing backward, legs spread carelessly, arms dangling, and head and neck bent forward in hard earnest concentration. He scratched his stubble and explained the situation with Yograj's corruption and the flyovers. He became animated as he spoke; he picked up his fork and jiggled it around; the table grew dense as everyone leaned in. The children were thrilled by this insider information. They salivated like journalists at an exclusive press conference. Even Arjun listened closely, slowly jabbing his butter knife between the quadrants of his outstretched hand. Despite himself, he felt proud of his father for his reasoning, and even prouder that he could present his father's morally charged resignation to Aarti, who, no doubt, would be impressed. He'd even act as ponderous as his Papa when he told her the news. Unconsciously and silently he began repeating under his breath everything his Papa was saying.

He was clicked out of the trance when his father said, rather abruptly, "Also. I have been thinking about the way all of you behave. We are all used to talking back to our elders in this house—enough of this. From today it is going to stop. Everyone will listen to their elders, okay? Do exactly as you are told. If your elder does something bad to you, then write me a letter of complaint. I will fix the problem. But no talking back."

Orders were orders, especially in a time of such tragedy. The children bent their heads especially low and chewed, for once, with their mouths closed. Only Sangita's cucumber crunching proceeded at its usual volume, but even this Mr. Ahuja didn't bother to correct. He still needed to tell her what had happened with Arjun.

But first he went to his study and placed a phone call to Vineet Yograj.

"Vineet saahb?" he said.

"Ah, Rakesh-ji," said Yograj. He sounded tired and expectant. As if he, too, had bad news to share.

Mr. Ahuja launched forth, "Look, ji, I am sure you have received the letter. Before you say anything, I want you to know I did not write it. I hundred percent did not write it. This is Rupa-ji's doing, I am certain. She has written it to promote infighting. The good woman has lost her mind, as you know. I am just now coming from seeing her. She has lost her mind. This is her—"

Mr. Ahuja cut himself off, not because he was finished but because he was surprised by the placidity of Yograj's attitude at the other end of the line, his patience, his lack of aggressive interruption.

"Yograji-ji?"

"Rupa-ji has done it, no?" Yograj said. "Why is she doing this? What is her problem? Does she not have better things to do? This is what I also thought." He shouted to his wife, off the phone, "Rekha! It is as I said. He did not write it. Why would he write it? Yes, exactly, Rakesh-ji, that is also what I thought. Why would you write it?"

Rakesh braced himself. "Yes."

He heard the wife utter a few shrill remarks but couldn't make them out.

"Sorry-ji," said Yograj. "That was my good wife. Please ignore. You understand, she is disturbed? But, yes, I also thought, Rakesh-ji is such a technocrat, how could he write this? Why would he write this? For what purpose? For what need? Why so much anger?"

"Yes," Rakesh mumbled.

He hadn't expected Yograj to believe him. He hadn't expected it to be so easy.

In fact, it wasn't. Because after a few notes of desultory conversation, Yograj said, "Will you do one thing for me, Rakesh-ji?" His voice was now commanding and smooth, not the gruff rattly voice he used for questions. "Will you please write a letter to the party as a whole and say you did not write the letter, and that it is the work of Rupa-ji? Just so they know? So my good name is not blemished?"

Yograj's good name. It came as a great surprise to Mr. Ahuja (though it shouldn't have) that Yograj cared less about their mutual enmity and more about what others in the party thought of him. Mr. Ahuja's comments had actually hurt him because they were so close to the truth. Immediately, the warm kindly feeling he'd started experiencing—the same feeling of forgiveness that overcame him after he slapped one of his children—was replaced by a sense of power. The slap had been necessary, and he was ready to deliver another.

Mr. Ahuja grinned broadly. "Okay, ji, whatever you desire," he said.

Then he hung up the phone, switched on his computer in the study, wrote out a note to Yograj, and told him, in so many words, to go screw himself and his good name.

CHAPTER 22

LOVE-SHOVE

MR. AHUJA'S CAREER with the KJSZP(H202) was now emphatically over—he had no allies to speak of—but he was in an exuberant mood as he walked to the nursery. Behind him were the Flyover Fast-Track and its failures. The flyovers could look bombed and ruined, the ramparts of a city abandoned after a pillage, and he wouldn't care. Years from now, he imagined, when archaeologists unearthed Delhi's ruins, they'd find inexplicable bridges. We have several hypotheses, they'd say. *People climbed up here to experience ritual hallucinations of tar . . . There is some proof that this is where salvos were fired at the Muslim invaders approaching from the Aravalli Mountain range . . . These were their temples, austere.*

If Delhi, as people loved to say, was a city of ruins, then at least his ruins towered over the rest.

"Everything is okay?" he asked, opening the door into Sangita's den. His manner was courtly, servile, his hands fanned in front of him like the mascot for Air India.

Mrs. Ahuja was noncommittal as she strung all the smelly nappies on a cord that stretched across the room. "All the babies are crying," she said. Then, by way of explanation: "Doing latrine."

The magic of marriage. Mr. Ahuja hadn't changed diapers in several months, but he was so grateful to see that Sangita was watching a soap opera and not NDTV—which no doubt would carry news of the latest developments—that he blitzkrieged through the nursery, turning the babies on their stomachs and sliding out the safety pins with panache. He mollified the infants with his old trick—a clicking of fingernails near their ears. Sangita watched the minister, fascinated. Mr. Ahuja felt at ease. His cell phone was vibrating in his pocket, a situation that only exacerbated his growing sexual frustration by alerting the nerves leading up to his penis. What attracted him about his wife right now as she cradled one of the twins in her lap was this: she was so available. He could suffer through the worst misfortunes in the world, and she'd be forced to stay with him. He could quit politics and still she'd be subordinate to him. He could lose the SPM's patronage and be instantly axed from the party for his irreverent letter, and she'd still shyly fan the dupatta near her face when he asked her questions. He, too, would stand up to his antagonizers like a man—he wouldn't make it easy for them. If they issued him a Show Cause Notice, he'd file a Breach of Privilege Motion in Parliament. He'd make such inflammatory remarks in the press that the Communist Party would back him in the creation of a Third Front. He'd explain everything to the press. The English-speaking press would like his good English. The Hindi-speaking press would like his good Hindi. They'd carry photographs of him with a fresh red tilak on his forehead, his showered bulk wrapped in a fancy kurta . . .

"Why are you watching MTV?" he asked. "Don't you know your age?"

"I have declared ban on StarPlus," she explained. "Because of—"

"Mohan Bedi?"

"Mohan Bedi."

"Well, stop worrying—your Mohan Bedi is going to live," he said to Sangita.

Sangita had now put the baby down and was sitting on a stool with a hot-water bottle flopped across her lap, one hand pressed on the side table for support, so that even the act of relaxation looked grueling.

"But he is dead," she said.

"Yes, yes, but he will be alive tomorrow."

"How will he be alive? He died in tub. Body was shown. Cell-o-phone was shown."

"Tcch. What is the problem? His twin died. The twin was in the tub," he bullshitted, "instead of Mohan. Twist of fate."

"He had no twin, ji."

"What do you mean—*how did he get in*? You have not seen two people in a tub? Brothers were bathing together, Mohan went outside to get soap, left the phone in the tub."

"But, ji—"

"Sangita," he said, suddenly, "I've told him."

Sangita tried not to blink. When Arjun had asked last night if she had "tricked" Mr. Ahuja, she'd consoled herself by thinking: *At least he still thinks I am his real mother.* Now that consolation was lost. She was confident that Arjun hated her.

Normally she'd have cried, but she felt she owed Mr. Ahuja nothing. She stalled. "Ji, told who? Told Shankar to make tea? Told postman to send post?"

"Sangita! I've told Arjun. About his mother," Mr. Ahuya said. Then, stroking her hair, "Sorry."

"Thank you," she said. Then she began knitting again.

Mr. Ahuja sputtered, "I did it for you. I told him you had been a very good mother. I told him nothing will be different. I told him he had to know, but the past is the past. I hope that is okay. I am sorry. But you only wanted me to tell him—"

Sangita nodded. "Yes, ji. Thank you." She smiled. That was the end.

"Has he told you anything?"

She shook her head.

Mr. Ahuja was understandably abashed as he made for the door. Sangita had taken the news so well that he felt even more guilty about having concealed from her the fact that he'd told Arjun about the "switch." He'd acted as if he'd done her a favor when, in fact, he'd cheated her. He ought to have sunk to his knees and apologized. He ought to make it up to her—but how? He knew nothing about this woman, this wife of fifteen-odd years. Vague details, yes—the tough jackfruits of her elbows, the sullen hump of her jaw, the bulbous nose she had proudly passed on to each child except for Arjun, TV, clean clothes, T-series cassettes, a fierce protection of her Right to Eat at the table—but nothing more. He twisted and turned in his head the Rubik's cube of domestic details and arrived at no sustainable patterns. His mind was a drawer rummaged of all its contents. He remembered what Rashmi always told him, *I used to be really afraid of dying until I was in love, I thought who will have known me if die,* those oddly prescient words, though of course a person's entire life became an arrow of prophecies once they passed, he knew that, and Sangita had probably never loved anyone in her life and she would die as vaguely as she had lived. Sangita was a symbol, a darkness. When she died, she would be dead, completely gone. As Rashmi tended to zero in his mind, so did Sangita. One day they would both explode into nothingness, and Mr. Ahuja pictured himself an old man bathed in fog, surrounded only by his children. But no, here he was—at the threshold of the nursery—years before the event.

Like a true slave of marriage, he would have to go down on his knees and ask his children what his wife truly loved.

Mr. Ahuja shuddered as he heard Sangita transmitting thicker and thicker strands of dissatisfaction between the twin antennae of her needles. He was back in the hotel room the morning after his wedding, waking to an empty bed, the bride gone, his illusion of complete control utterly zapped, his misogynies exploded, the sheets on the bed crinkled with newborn peaks and valleys: He was deeply despicable, awful, self-centered. He was thinking: *I deserve no better than this woman. If I find her outside, I will marry her. I will marry her and treat her kindly.*

But still he was thinking only of himself.

"I love you," Mr. Ahuja said, ludicrously, turning around. He walked confidently toward Sangita, arms swinging.

Sangita now was truly shocked. She bent down from the stool and picked up a ball of yarn and stuck a needle through it. She blew her nose loudly on a napkin.

Mr. Ahuja got down on his knees before her stool and said it again, "I love you."

She brought a fold of her nighty up to her face and soaked it in tears.

Mr. Ahuja loomed over her with his nostrils quivering. "I love you darling. We have been through very difficult times together. You have been a good wife. Come. Let me take you to a film today. We'll go to the movies. Anything you want."

Mr. Ahuja made at least ten more promises he wouldn't keep, but it worked: she got up and stood in his arms. She let Mr. Ahuja do what he wanted. She limply put her head on his shoulder. She let him grope her fetching protuberance. She let him go erect against the overhang of her stomach. She knew he was lying and that she'd be disappointed—these were tears of loss, not joy—but she had waited so many years to hear these words that she didn't care. She let him stand there and be a man. Mr. Ahuja was grateful for her cooperation, for her warmth; he held her tighter and tighter. Soon the gratefulness became pride. He felt proud that he'd stood his ground, that he hadn't stormed off, that he'd told Arjun the secret, that he was holding his wife amidst the mewls of his offspring, lying to her for *her* sake. Let Arjun walk in on him now, he thought. Let Arjun gawk at him now. He was in a compromising position, but at least it resembled affection.

CHAPTER 23

THE WRONG BUS STOP

THE AHUJA EARLY MORNING Waking Undertaking was a fragile hierarchy. This is how it worked: Rakesh woke the oldest child; and then the oldest child woke the next; and so on until there was a huge queue forming outside the two bathrooms for a speedy brush-bath-shit-and-breakfast, a rowdy routine marred by toothbrush duels and the sound of slippers thwacking angrily against doors that were locked too long. Everyone got five minutes; and you bathed on alternate days, substituting the snow of talcum powder for soap, and heaven forbid if you tried to break the rules, there'd be shouting and the rehearsed revenge of your siblings to pay, they'd radar your movements through the day and prevent you from using the bathroom even if you were caught in the dire throes of shit, and then what? You'd have to run out into the street and make a beeline for the bushes.

Sangita's role in the organization was that of first pisser (special quota for pregnant ladies!) and final checker (once a week). She'd stand at the door, examine each sleepy tie, brush the lint off the children's shoulders (even if it meant standing on her toes for the boys), hand them their hotfoiled-parathas, and finally put her chubby hand to the small of their backs and shove them out of the house one by one, Rakesh included. So, Sangita might have been at the bottom of the chain, but she was the one who gave the go-ahead, the all-clear, the *Sayonara baby*, and if she noticed that anything was amiss or that one of the kids was dripping snot onto his or her white uniform she could choke the entire convoy, bring all progress to a halt, and mop the nosey crowd with a giant hanky.

But progress had been halted much earlier today. Mr. Ahuja hadn't woken up.

It was just his luck, thought Arjun, that he couldn't even go to school. Through no fault of his own he had missed the bus and, by association, Aarti—the only vision that could possibly comfort him, the only pair of eyes that could tell him, in the Morse code of fluttering eyelashes, *It'll be okay*. He wanted to see her to be convinced that he wouldn't be disgusted by the thought of sex for the rest of his life; that Mama and Papa wouldn't pop up hideously in his mind like a Hallmark Card (paradoxically wholesome) whenever he tried to seduce a woman.

He checked his e-mail. There was no word from her.

So six hours after waking, having played the Metallica album *Master of Puppets* that Ravi had lent him yesterday—Arjun crept out of the teeming house. He wore his school uniform, took an auto all the way to St. Columba's and lurked on the other side of the road as the 1:45 P.M. bell went off. Then, whistling, hands in his pockets, Arjun boarded bus #21.

He sat in the back of the bus, in the middle of the wide seat that afforded him a view down the aisle. He watched as a gaggle of seniors from the Convent of Jesus and Mary and St. Columba's made magnetically for the back—no Aarti. The junior school students all huddled in the front of the bus, shooting sharp glances backward every so often, trying to imagine what it would feel like to sit at the back, far from the driver and the teachers, playing Harry Potter and WWF trump cards with real money or flirting on the footboard, the rumble of traffic only inches from your feet. Arjun ruffled his hair, nervously waved to a boy from his class who said, *Oh so you were bunking class all day, good job, yaar.* The floor under him suddenly ignited, the engine roaring to life—and it was only then that Aarti climbed aboard, her dark mane of hair flustered around her neck, the satchel slung low on her waist like she could barely carry it. Oh, the sweaty beauty of it all. Arjun clutched his empty bag, now confident that his idea to reserve the seat next to him had paid off. That was the only spot left at the back, and Aarti would *have* to sit there.

He was wrong.

Aarti swung herself into a seat right at the front, shouldering up against a little boy who barely reached her shoulder. Then she promptly fell asleep.

On the bus, Aarti slept uncontrollably. She slept through everything—the imprecations of the conductor sitting ahead, the sputter of the bus's exhaust, the unbridled nose blowing of the little boy beside her, even the snap of her head on the axis of its neck as her body succumbed to centrifugality. If only Arjun could hold her head, stroke her hair, be—in other words—a *master* to her *puppet*. But the possibility of such manly rescue grew increasingly remote; Arjun's bus-stop sparkled in the distance, a slab of white-hot pavement. He tensed in his seat, and trapezed his butt over the worn plastic, instinctively readying himself to get off at Khan Market. But then his butt slammed back in place. He couldn't leave her like this, not after making the arduous journey just to speak to her. And, more importantly, what if no one woke her? What if she slept all the way to the bus depot, and the lecherous bus driver who chewed too much paan roused her, his hand conveniently on her left breast as he said, *Hello, baby, you are ishleeping?*

He couldn't let it happen. The bus trembled to a stop, unloaded its passengers, and then Arjun sighed as his stop was left behind, hopscotching toward the horizon. Arjun moved forward a few seats; a few minutes later, the boy sitting next to Aarti climbed over her cautiously, as if she was a rusty jungle gym, and then he, too, was gone.

Now there was only one problem: Arjun had no idea which stop was Aarti's. He had never ridden so far in the bus, wasn't it strange how you could travel in a bus for years and years and only know a small sliver of its route, the origins of your co-passengers a perpetual mystery only seconds away from being unmasked, and yet you did nothing about it—you simply stepped into a cloud of dust at the appointed place at the appointed time and never asked questions. Arjun wished he had asked questions, he wished he didn't have to use vague parameters like Aarti's command of English (which was rather good) and the stylishness of her backpack (which was rather big and bulky and ugly, signaling unhealthy ambition) to know when to wake her, and so he was acting purely on intuition when he came up behind her, tapped her on the shoulder with the romantic poise of a judge bringing down the gavel, said "Aarti, your stop is here," so causing her to startle out of sleep, notice immediately that the bus was stationary and snorting impatiently for her to depart, and bolt right down the stairs with the bag swinging behind her in a neat Olympian arc.

Arjun followed, hands thrust deep in his pockets, the metal boards thudding under his feet.

They faced each other on the dusty bus stop at Nizamuddin. Across from them, a two-storied tomb in the middle of a roundabout. Everything had a heightened vitality. A microcosm for the heat and temper of Delhi. The sky hurtling earthward, steamrolling the soft curve of the Golf Club Flyover in shimmer. The light gentle—not acidic, eye-shutting, traumatizing—a neutral pH of vision, the sun and the clouds deadening each other in pastel shades. Nothing loud. Nothing hurt. Nothing blinked. The sky had suffered a power cut; the branches tangling out from the plant shop behind them were burned wires; the giant tap-head of the blue tomb had been turned off by an arid hand.

He needed to piss badly. Aarti did not know this. *Or did she?*

Why else was she standing beside him with her head bowed slightly (as if to tame the gloriously upturned nose), arms crossed, sleeves pulled over her hands, the satchel-strap slashing between her breasts so that they bubbled up in her shirt?

Her hand finally windmilled on the axis of her wrist.

He needed to piss very badly.

"This isn't my bus stop," she said, smoothing her skirt.

Arjun panicked. "Oh shit! Fucking crap. I'm sorry. No one else got off so I thought—"

Then he ran after the bus.

"Wait!" she shouted behind him, rubbing the craters of sleeplessness under her eyes.

But there was no time to lose. Arjun had rocketed off, his backpack bouncing on the small mound of his butt. As the bus slowed down at the next red light, he leaped over the jamun-wallah on the sidewalk, felt an ice-cream wrapper snag around his foot, and suddenly found himself being jerked into the shell of his backpack with the violent pullback action of a slingshot. It was Aarti. Aarti holding him by his shoulder straps. Gentle, patient Aarti. He could feel her breathing on his shoulder. He wanted to knot the floppy sleeves of her shirt, keep her close like this. She let go of him like a bully who has suddenly seen the face of reason or a schoolteacher.

"Sorry," she whispered, as he turned to face her, "I didn't want to make—to make a scene." This was new to Arjun. To not want to make a scene. To go to such lengths to not make a scene. Unheard of. Undiscovered. Like a cure for cancer or a salve for the Indian cricket team's bad performance. Like a private piddle that bothered no one.

"I got you into this, I feel bad," he said, thighs now squeezed together in agony. "I'll call my car. My driver can drop you."

"This isn't your bus stop?" she asked, yawning.

"No," he said.

"Oh right—" she said, shelving neat strands of hair behind her ears. Her face was beautiful in a way that confounded photographs, a canvas where expressions achieved a profound fixity, a smile or a nervous crimping of the forehead like a thing that could last forever. You could tell she knew this about her face; her hands were always snaky and articulate near her mouth; the arch of her fingers seemed to lead to the prized lips.

"I have some work around here," he said.

"I'll get a taxi," she said. "I'll feel bad if you feel bad, so don't worry about it, okay?"

"But why?" he asked. Then he had an idea. "My car can come any time. I have just one minute work in the plant shop, will you hold my bag?"

She did as she was told mostly because she was in shock, and before she could respond, he had dropped his backpack at her feet with a resounding thump and legged it through the green gates.

• • •

He entered the RC Kataria Plant Shop.

He returned minutes later with a potted tulsi plant and a still-full bladder.

This, however, had not been the plan.

The plan had been to skirt across the broken concrete floor crisscrossed by leafy shadows, observe the glorious mess of foliage, and find a bubble bath of rhododendrons to piss into. But the gardener, dressed in a spare dhoti and writing in a notebook, had viewed the schoolboy suspiciously and chased him all the way out of the plant shop with his eyes—preventing him from pissing and guilting Arjun into buying a plant that he now held out to Aarti by means of apology, the red pot feeling cold in his hands, the mud in the pot dark and gloomy like the inside of Aarti's pupils.

"What's this, Arjun?" she asked, standing on her toes. "Are you on your school's green brigade?" She let on nothing about last night's e-mail.

"Oh, that's the work I had," he said with great effort, as if the words were a dam across a lake of piss. "To buy a plant. For a science project. On photosynthesis. And fluorescence—"

"Arjun, actually I think I'll take a cab," she said. "I have FIITJEE soon, and I just called my parents on my mobile to tell them I'll go straight there. Thanks so much for offering, though."

"Can I offer you this plant?" he said with a goofy grin.

"Taxi!" she shouted.

Arjun couldn't believe it: Was she really going to leave? If yes, why lead him on and touch him and hold him by the backpack straps for this? He was irritated and upset, particularly because he still needed to piss and because the entire problem of pissing could have been solved easily by . . . an erection. Courtesy of Aarti. An erection always stalled piss. He wished now that Aarti was more forthright and sexual, that her body offered up more of itself than it did—she was cute and affectionate and was sticking out her hip to hail a taxi, but that was all, the convent girls' uniform made her seem formless, it wasn't good enough to erase the memory of his parents making love two nights ago. Standing in the plant shop, he had felt the same way, imagining his parents in the bamboo grove, their bodies like two lush, large leaves, skin that shriveled to the touch, only tiny spots of perspiration reflecting off the foliage.

He wanted to see Aarti naked, was the thing. He wanted to grab hold of her hand, feel the veins piping the underside of her arm, fling the potted plant in the middle of the Nizamuddin roundabout so that the exploding shards forced the spirals of cars to widen and let them pass, both of them clambering into the blue tomb that sat at the base of the Golf Club Flyover, where he would finally kiss her, feel his way toward the dead bed of the gravestone, and say, "Do you want to start a riot?" referring of course to the fact that his penis was circumcised and outwardly Muslim and she was a Hindu, and if they had been having sex in a tense Hindu-Muslim area, their union might have triggered off communal riots, in fact the sex would be so amazing that there would certainly be riots, all sorts of people would die, new tombs would sprout up across the city, more places to dally in—

"You really should be careful about the taxis these days," he whispered to her. "Most of the drivers are Ms."

"Ms?" she asked.

"Muslims!" he said, and then looked around to see if the throng of passing Muslim boys—all dressed in tight white caps and gray kurtas—had heard. They had just crossed the road from the Nizamuddin Dargah, the Muslim shrine.

Aarti looked irritated. "Look, Arjun, that's silly. This is the middle of Delhi. It's the most boring place in the world. Nothing like that could happen. Nothing ever happens in Delhi. And if you ask me, our Hindu driver-types are the worst. These Muslims at least respect their women—"

"That's true," said Arjun. He felt chastised. "I'm only saying because—okay. I don't want you to go."

She thought for a moment. She bit her lower lip.

"Stay," he said, "I like you."

It appeared, for once, that he had said the right thing. She said quickly, "I like you too." Then: "But have you seen this part of Delhi? It's my favorite part of Delhi. Everything else is so boring. Here at least there is culture."

He looked enviously at two men unzipping side-by-side under a giant keekar tree. He admired the gall of the peanut seller who was scratching his pelvis. The city at crotch level was where he belonged. He put the tulsi plant on the ground to commemorate the beginning of his relationship with Aarti.

"Let's go for a walk," she said.

Walking was good. Walking fast was better. It kept his bladder dancing. He used Aarti's cell phone to call home and asked that Balwant Singh bring the car to Nizamuddin, and yes he was fine, he was just buying a plant, he'd be right back, okay bye.

Then he clicked the phone off and turned to Aarti and started talking about the band. He told her how they'd forged a signature rock style on the flyover. How they'd one-upped their competition by choosing as their summit a place still swirling with searchlights of dust and dampness; how the passing cars had all plunked gravel into the dicey-looking pits below. She was duly impressed, and said, "Where do you practice regularly?"

"On a flyover, yaar," said Arjun.

Suddenly the band name was clear to him: The Flyover Yaars. The next day in school he presented it to his band-mates amid much fanfare; the four boys threw themselves into the project of mythmaking. They broadcast freely to their classmates about their bold shenanigans on the Godse Nagar Flyover. Drew diagrams of musical levitation on the blackboard that shimmered at noon, chalky pulsars radioactive with rumors. Preached the legend of the band to the white-uniformed masses. Were even felicitated with free offerings of slimy chow mein in the canteen, which they set on fire to see if they truly contained petrol, as the popular legend went. But there was no soy-blaze, no biohazard, only extra-charred noodles.

Aarti said, "Here we are."

They entered the shanty through a narrow alley smeared with slush. On either side were tiny shacks serving tea and huge fluffy naans and rotis. Men glanced at them as they reached with giant spears into the glowing cylinders of their tandoors. Goats strained at their tethers; Aarti reached out to pet one. All around Arjun were alien-looking signs in Urdu: Muslim bookstores, Waqf boards, tube-light shops. The men and women in the area appeared to be staring at Aarti, her bare knees poking forward into the dusty afternoon light. Yet she was utterly un-self-conscious. Arjun walked a little behind her, both hands dug into his back pant-pockets.

He was squeezing his butt to hold in the piss. It appeared, strangely, to work.

"Don't you love that this is the middle of Delhi?" she said. "All these women in burkhas and all these beautiful dilapidated buildings. But wait till you go into the dargah. Sometimes they have qawallis here. It's really amazing. Do you know how old this is?"

To Arjun it all just seemed poor. They entered a quadrangular space between buildings and stood at the edge of a tank filled with water. Children were climbing up to the precarious ledges of the buildings, hanging their shirts on the spikes of TV antennae and then diving down into the tank as if this were the most natural thing in the world. They screamed and cursed. In the dappled light Arjun studied Aarti's reflection in the water, only to have it shattered with a splash. They both stepped back.

"The culture is so rich," Aarti continued. "What do we Hindus have in Delhi? It's really boring being a Hindu. All the temples—well, except Hanuman Mandir—were built like two days ago. And then we don't have any strict traditions. You can do what you want and you don't have to do what you don't want. That's why I get bored when my Dadi goes to the temple. I know nothing bad will happen if I don't pray." She sighed. "Do you know—sometimes I wish I was a Muslim."

"Well—"

"What? You think I'm weird?" she said, bobbing her satchel up in defiance.

"No—you're damn boring."

"Shut up." She giggled.

"But can I tell you a secret?" said Arjun.

They passed through an arch into the main courtyard of the dargah. It was unremarkable to Arjun. It looked like the inside of one of those long filthy tiled old Delhi kothis that his father sometimes visited to massage constituents and local chieftains. In the middle of the courtyard was a tiny tomb.

"What?" said Aarti.

"Promise you won't tell anyone?"

"Yes—"

"I was born a Muslim," Arjun blurted.

She didn't know what to make of this. In the shadows of the buildings her face was softened; he felt he could reach out and touch it and it might fall through his fingers like a curl of smoke.

"I mean. I'm like them"—he nodded toward the boys diving from ledges—"down there. I'm circumscribed. I mean, circumcised. Sorry, am I disturbing you? No? Good. We are adults; we can say these things. But I was adopted by a Hindu family. That's why I never tell you about my family. I'm actually adopted. My real mother died when I was three."

He had said it and yet the statement seemed curiously lacking in weightiness. He himself could feel nothing for Rashmi; he had lost only an abstraction.

"I'm so sorry," she said.

"It's okay. I'm a stepson—I've always been treated like one. I have twelve brothers and sisters, and I'm forced to do all the work and take care of them. That's why I needed to start this band. So I could escape."

"You have twelve brothers and sisters?"

"Yes. Yes. Yes. I've never told anyone. I don't know why I'm telling you."

Here is where the plan went awry for Arjun. His eyes began to redden with tears.

Aarti said, "Are you okay, Arjun?"

They were standing side by side at the threshold of the shrine with the outer edges of her satchel and his backpack pressing against each other. She was close enough that he could smell sharpened pencils and shampoo and face cream. But she hadn't turned to face him. Her shoulders had gone stiff. She was teasing and coiling her hair nervously with both hands. She was at a loss. She was looking left and right.

"Are you okay, Arjun?" she said.

"Yes, I'm fine," he growled. "Sorry. Let's go. My car will be almost here."

They started walking back out in rapid steps. Why was he crying? Was it scientifically possible that piss held in on one end could become tears on the other? His throat and nose and sinuses felt coated with crushed glass. Then they were back on the main road, back in the hubbub. He'd stopped crying but was still sniffling, and she turned to him again and said, "Arjun, how long have you known? That you were adopted?" She was looking at her feet.

Arjun said, "I don't want to talk about it. Sorry."

"Okay, sorry."

"No, no, no, it's okay."

Now they waited at the bus stop in silence. He stepped into her shadow on the peanut-strewn pavement. Inside, he fumed and fumed and fumed. Why had he chosen to tell her such a huge, stupid lie? *I was born a Muslim, I've been treated like a stepson*. Great! Now he could never have the band and the family and Aarti in the same place. He could never organize a concert. His life was compartmentalized beyond repair. No one—not even Aarti, the girl to whom he'd wished to confess everything—would know who he truly was.

No one would know, Arjun thought, that there wasn't much to know.

There it was, that hideous self-pity, and his eyes began to redden again in defense, and so it was a great relief when he saw the car thundering through the traffic toward them, the way he loved it—siren ablaze, the government-spoke on the hood fluttering in slipstreams, windows tinted as if to protect a supermodel from the paparazzi. He enjoyed the pomp and ceremony of a government car, the way an Ambassador—an ungainly, diesel beast—changed into the ultimate symbol of plush power as soon as it was fitted with a siren. He liked the way the drawl of the car's approach took people by surprise; how they tried hard to not ask, *Is your Papa in the government?* And how they always failed as soon as the powerful AC blast knocked them flat against the cool leather upholstery.

Unfortunately, he had told her already about his father. There was no element of surprise left.

So when the car arrived, he refused to get in. The driver, Balwant, had rolled down the window and said, "Oye, Handsome," and he hated that. He hated being called *handsome* or *hero*.

"I have to buy another plant," he explained to Aarti as she got in the back. "For my science project. I don't know why I put it down."

"Maybe it's here still?" she said, half out of the car.

"It's gone," Arjun said, ruefully.

She didn't believe him, didn't believe he needed to buy a plant; he could tell. She mussed her hair with both her hands, then dropped one hand to adjust her stockings—economizing on the action by bending down and doing a graceful half-turned wave—the other hand still coiling strands around the fingers, releasing shiny ring after ring of hair.

Arjun turned to the driver. "Balwant, please drop madam to Defence Colony."

Then he slammed the door and watched the car rev away. A blizzard of dust caped after the car and covered his tongue with soot. He was stranded in a flickering daytime slot of Delhi, a soap opera that no one wanted to watch. Cars and cows and scooters passed him by. They didn't even honk. How peculiar to be pandering to an audience of one. How tiring, draining, terrifying. He parked himself before a keekar tree and took a piss that lasted several generations, his legs splayed out in a broad V. He felt pleasantly crushed; his bladder pistoned with relief; his old optimism returned. What had happened today was private. Mama would never find out what he'd said about her, and to cancel his sins, he'd go home and prove to her that she was more than an enforced intermission in his increasingly-cinematic life. He'd be a good son. He'd do something special for her. Offer a free massage. Or buy her VCDs. Or better still, take her to watch a movie.

As a result of this altruistic scheming, he wasn't quite ready for the news that awaited him at home.

CHAPTER 24

THE NEWS AT HOME

THE HOUSE WAS UNDER SIEGE: dozens of men and women had settled in the driveway and were squatting on either side of the phalanx of dozing ministerial cars, newspapers twisted over their heads against the relentless sun. They were either constituents (they wore the hassled expressions of people who've asked their minister to install water pumps in their villages one too many times) or money men (hassled in general). The garden, meanwhile, was surrounded by a rampart of speakers. Into its denuded pliant mud had been plunged wooden posts, and from the wooden posts was hung a massive, gaudy, maroon tent. It was the same brand of tent one saw at weddings, some macabre dusty sheet patterned with arabesques, and it was beneath this tent, in awesome shade, that Mr. Ahuja sat on a chair in a white kurta getting his hair cut. He was old-fashioned that way. He kept his eyes closed and smacked his lips as the barber snipped at his hair with exaggerated karate-style chops. His hair looked wrong and jagged, but even more disconcerting was the red rose Mr. Ahuja held daintily in his hand between thumb and forefinger, sniffing it every time his barber came to the end of a sequence of chops. The barber was not much older than Arjun and so stopped respectfully when he saw him approaching.

Mr. Ahuja opened his eyes; they were bloodshot in a regal, Mughal way.

"What is all this, Papa?" Arjun said.

Even as he asked, he thought: *a concert. He is making up for yesterday by organizing a concert.*

Mr. Ahuja said, "Beta, I understand this is very sudden. But we are going to have to move in one month's time from this house. So I wanted to have a party at the earliest. Tomorrow night."

"We're going to move? What do you mean?"

Mr. Ahuja sat upright. "Look. As you know, I have resigned—"

"But, Papa—"

"And not only have I resigned. But, for once, my resignation has been accepted!" Mr. Ahuja chuckled unconvincingly. "And thus we will move."

They were living in a government-sanctioned home, a VIP accommodation.

"But, Papa, I thought you said the government will also fall. If the government falls, then can't you keep the house till the next election?"

"Come again?"

"I THOUGHT YOU SAID THE GOVERNMENT WILL ALSO FALL."

"Who says the government is falling? There is a Sixth Front being formed between Rupa Bhalla and the CPI. I thought Yograj was also going to withdraw and so the government would collapse. But this is not happening. And I have decided to stand by my decision. Sometimes one must do the thing that is morally right."

"You'll still be a Member of Parliament I thought. Even if you are not in the government you're an MP, right? As an MP you can keep the house."

Mr. Ahuja was impressed by his son's interrogation. He said so. "Very sharp you've become, eh? Look, the situation is this. I will be frank. This house we are living in is bigger and better, more spacious than the house of any other MP. Do you know why? Because we are staying in the house that was allotted for Rupa Auntie. I am only leasing the house from her. So now that she and I are no longer on talking terms, she will cancel the lease. I know her too well. We will have to move. We have no choice."

Arjun dug his hands into his pockets. How to explain to Papa that Rupa Auntie could have taken away the house (the sacred birth place of nearly half his siblings), the garden (the burial ground of soiled diapers), and the guards, and it would all have been fine, if only there was a way to preserve the bus route that came bowtied to this prime location? He'd have to change buses if he changed neighborhoods, and then there'd be no Aarti to unwrap every morning or to festoon with offerings of wit. To think he'd only been moody with her today because he knew he could remedy it tomorrow with sniveling kindness and a Bryan Adams reference. What if there was no tomorrow. What if this was the end. Hello, Good-bye. His massive, smooth forehead contorted with suppressed speech; Mr. Ahuja could sense it.

"Look, beta," he continued, "I know this is very difficult to swallow. It is very difficult for me also. Put yourself in my shoes. But we will get over this. In fact, you must play an active role at this party tomorrow. I will introduce you around. And you can even perform with your band if you like. We can turn the party into a concert."

"No. We're not good. The band's not good."

"Of course you are."

"You don't know what good music is."

"That is not your concern," said Mr. Ahuja. He brushed off a few darts of hair that were poking out of his shoulder. "I will arrange that."

"How is it not *my* concern if *I* am playing?"

"Arjun, please. Why would you pay? You asked me if I had provided food and booze, and I said yes."

"Ah, Papa! I said, You have no idea WHAT GOOD MUSIC IS."

Mr. Ahuja laughed at himself. "Yes, you're right. I'm sorry."

"I'm sorry too."

Arjun looked away from his father and scratched his cheek. He was surprised by his stubble and scratched some more.

Mr. Ahuja persisted. "Arjun, have the concert. You can even invite the girl you like. The one who goes on your bus?"

Arjun wanted to hand it to the man—he had a marvelous sense of timing and an unlimited number of informants, how could he possibly know about an insignificant bus romance?—but then the source of the information came to him in a thunderclap of consciousness: his siblings. They'd betrayed him, the bastards. They'd pay for this.

"There are many girls who go on the bus, Papa," he said. "They are *all* my girlfriends.When the right time is there, I will invite all of them. You can help me choose even."

"But your brothers and sisters told me—"

"Forgot what they say, Papa. They're all liars. They have nothing better to do but tell lies about me. They're stepbrothers and stepsisters, and they want to have a stepsister-in-law. This is the sort of thing I have to deal with all the time. Maybe I should also resign. Will you accept my resignation? I resign."

Arjun had intended to sound joke-y, but the last two lines were spat out; his tongue hissed and flickered between his teeth.

Mr. Ahuja said, "Very funny, let me consider it," and tittered uneasily. He was not a man much given to tittering.

After Arjun stomped his way back to the house, Mr. Ahuja sat in the chair under the tent and massaged his head. He beckoned the barber over and had him point a giant industrial fan at his face. The brutal surge of wind was suffocating, but the trick was done: the shorn hair was sucked off his face and shoulders and nose and into a minor jetstream that plummeted and scattered into the camouflaging greenery of the garden. Still he prickled from his recent snipping; he had sensitive skin; he felt the full weight of Arjun's immaturity. It appeared to Mr. Ahuja that Arjun was setting himself dangerously against the family. Already he considered them step-relations. He wasn't doing well at school or at home or with his band. He needed to be distracted away from this zoo, or more trouble was in store. There was only one place for him, Mr. Ahuja decided with a sigh, there was no point denying it, and so when he entered the house, he took Arjun aside from the dining table where he sat peering dumbly into a notebook—a rare scene of homework-in-progress—and said, "I have thought about your proposition."

"I'm sorry, Papa" said Arjun. "I was only joking."

"No, no, it's okay. You will not *resign* or any such thing, but you have to help me with the next campaign. What do you say? You will be one of my political advisers. Tonight you'll come with me to a function. You'll be my right-hand man. What do you say?"

Looks of pure thrill are rare: Arjun's face became a singularity, a thing invented solely to fulfill the promise of the moment, all of the self and its self-consciousness and history obliterated by the delicate dance of muscles that signify wonder. He forgot all about helping Mama as he'd planned; he forgot even, for a moment, about Aarti and his siblings and his homework. He looked like a baby, he was a baby. *He's not cynical, he'll have to be taught everything from scratch*, thought Mr. Ahuja, and even though he knew he was inviting disaster—even though he knew that the two of them could never get along—he felt glad. He'd done the right thing.

"Are you serious, Papa?"

"What do you say?"

"Yes, Papa," gasped Arjun. "Of course, yes, Papa."

Then the disasters began.

EPILOGUE

THE DISASTER

THE DISASTERS IN THE YEARS THAT FOLLOWED were too numerous to mention; like the sputterings of a dying engine or the jarring contractions of pregnancy, they varied in duration and heat and oomph and involved fistfights, property deals, disownings, rekindlings, namecallings, many many babies, and the occasional furious riot; and they continued till the very day Mr. Ahuja retired twenty years later from the Congress (I) Party (to which he had uneasily defected), willing his constituency and collected clout to Arjun.

But the most lasting disaster was the very first one. It occurred shortly after the Ahujas moved, and it was such a disaster that, like the popular election of an autocrat or the slippage of a cruel clause into a civil law, it didn't even seem like one.

As Mr. Ahuja had promised, there was indeed a final party at the residence on Modi Estate Road. Politicians of all stripes were invited home. In the heat of April they ran amok on the bronzed grass of the backyard garden, undeterred: bottlebrushes bobbing overhead; gravity pulling the devalued gold currency of leaves from the seemingly infinite treasury of trees; cool cloud shadows appearing and then scudding away. The men and women mingled in ferocious patterns around snack servers and stopped dead as the hydra of Arjun's siblings approached and swallowed them in a ritual of foot-touching and uncle-how-are-yous and auntie-will-you-have-another-whiskeys. Giant five-foot industrial fans blew hair back in gorgeous candy-floss swirls. The garden sounded like a helipad: the people, shouting in compensation, looked their natural extremes. Bald men got windy combovers, lone strands wipering their shiny pates, and women who had spent hours dyeing themselves a stylish salt-and-pepper found white bluffs foaming up without warning.

It was through this scene that Mr. Ahuja pranced with a drink in either hand, enacting a new level of aggression, speaking freely, being boisterous and gruff, sharking after the chicken tikkas and kathi rolls and mushrooms and whatnots. It was as if he'd forgotten he was the host. He was enjoying politics again.

Arjun, too, was enjoying politics. He drank too much and shook hands with an army general who gripped his right hand so tight that he couldn't turn a tap for days (or masturbate) and flirted with a woman twice his age and then puked into a bed of salvias in the garden.

But none of this was disastrous. Nor was the fact that Aarti grew increasingly tired on the morning ride, escaping from Arjun daily on the checkerboard of seats on the bus; that he got used to thinking of her not as a girl he liked but as a flickering Polaroid that was destined to fade till it was no more and he boarded a new bus in a new life in an era of utter darkness; or that the band, the Flyover Yaars, met two times in a cavernous auditorium to practice and came to the simultaneous conclusion that they sounded like a chorus of eunuchs demanding money at a marriage; or even that Ravi called Arjun up one morning and said, "You won't believe what happened," and Arjun said, "What?" and Ravi said, "That girl we hit in the car died. Complications, yaar," and Arjun sobbed like a baby for a minute—What are friends for if you can't sob in front of them?—until Ravi told him he was only joking, man, and did he want to go with him to give flowers to that babe?

"My Dad wants me to do it," he explained.

Arjun refused and was more than a little sharp with Ravi. And still nothing bad happened. Ravi just cackled and cackled and told him another story. The friendship was sustained. The band became for a while a complex in-joke, mentioned with smoky guffaws when they stood in a secret alcove behind the basketball court during games period and traded cigarettes.

None of this was disastrous.

Then the ministerial lease on the house expired, and one

obscenely sunlit July morning—after what had seemed like a month of textile milling (Sangita, do we really need to keep all fifty sweaters?), and shocking discoveries (the house shed carrom tokens like lice), and a protracted study of the graying polka dots running up and down the formerly white walls (What were these? Remnants of the days when Arjun and Varun played cricket inside the house and smacked the ball against the wall?)—the Ahujas were back in Rakesh's family home in Greater Kailash.

Here, things began to go sour. There wasn't enough space, it was a house made for four. It was a house as pressure cooker. The twin girls, Gita and Sonali, made a debut into the world of walking; they developed a fixation with the corked jar of mango preserves that sat in the storage room with a big rubber band tied around its glass top, and had to be shooed away from all the sharp corners by a team of bossy brothers. Mrs. Ahuja, meanwhile, was exiled to the lower-level of the two-storied house, where she lived a somewhat solitary existence, surrounded by servants whom she couldn't stand. The reason for the exile was that there were no bathrooms on the second floor, and her trips to the toilet were, as a side effect of her pregnancy, extremely frequent.

As for sex, there was none on either level. And there would be none.

Arjun and Mr. Ahuja were mostly absent. But most of their time was spent not on productive real-world tasks—in Mr. Ahuja's case, drinking with his financiers and moneymen or dashing off enraged letters to newfound nemeses; in Arjun's case, sweetly failing a math exam, making a botched but sincere attempt to impress girls with the story of his flyover follies, or daydreaming his way onto the new bus with eyes trained instinctively toward Aarti, who was missing, being troubled now no doubt by some other boy in an alternative cuboidal universe on wheels—but in a car together, fretting, fuming, getting nowhere.

Mr. Ahuja missed the simple pleasure of the red emergency siren on his official car—a siren he'd misused gloriously to part the civilian seas of the city. The traffic in Delhi had in the last few months gone from awful to horrendous. The first phase of the Flyover Fast-Track was over, but the flyovers were yet to be opened. They'd been built and painted and even tousled with greenery; what they lacked was inauguration.

It was a problem of protocol, then. A flyover could not be officially opened unless a minister came with an army of cronies and a coconut, and then had one of the cronies smash the coconut on the tarred ramp of the overpass. Easy enough, except there were no free ministers to speak of. The Mohan Bedi–Rupa Bhalla Government, or the Sixth Front, collapsed soon after Vineet Yograj realized that Prime Minister Mohan Bedi, despite his childishness, could not be bought or manhandled—he was rich and burly—and so decided to withdraw support, which was why the ministers had better things to do than throw coconuts at concrete.

In the weeks of confusion and electoral horse-trading that ensued, the citizens of Delhi grew tired of driving, waiting, crashing, honking, screaming, and generally drumming their fingers on the boiling dashboards of their dented cars.

Then, one day, a few vigilantes, aided by an activist TV channel, arrived at the Godse Nagar Flyover, removed—with great and exaggerated heaving-and-hoeing—the yellow police barriers blocking the ramp, and drove their scooters and motorcycles up and down the ridged road.

A point had been made, but it wasn't noted. The barriers were put back in place by the police, and the flyover slumbered again on the horizon. No one felt this was a disaster.

Except Mr. Ahuja. He couldn't take it anymore. He had tried to use the extra time in the car to whisper stories about Rashmi to Arjun (he gifted to his son the cricketer tie), but was soon convinced of the futility of these efforts. Having told the secret had made Rashmi recede even further, and what was the point of revisiting her simply to confirm the fact of his forgetting?

He began instead to complain constantly about the flyovers. He had a right to take the delay personally. "This is utter bosh," he said. And because Arjun was now Mr. Ahuja's right-hand man, he couldn't take it anymore either. "Yes, bosh," said Arjun.

This is when The Flyover Yaars had their second coming.

Ravi and Arjun and Anurag and Deepak began convening at the base of finished but unopened flyovers—cheered again by the same bored, activist TV channel—and began performing rejigged songs by Bryan Adams. "Summer of '69 Flyovers," and "Everything I Do (I Do It for a Flyover)" were among their notable numbers. Ravi was present because he'd been able to convince his father that not only could he get a college essay for U.S. universities out of this but he could also claim this was community service, which, actually, it was not. The Flyover Yaars were astonishingly bad. No one who heard them liked them, and most people didn't hear them at all. One critic described them as "listening to a man blow noisy balloon animals, except that he is still at the shape-choosing stage." Whatever that meant. They were all set-up and no follow-through. Here's why. Arjun would get up to the microphone and watch the slipstreams of passing cars chase plastic cups and tissues and bags of chips across the concrete and imagine he was in a slow-motion MTV music video. Behind him, Ravi would rotate endlessly in his asteroid belt of drums; Deepak would double further and further into himself as he freed a grueling solo from his Stratocaster; and Anurag, hunched over his keyboard, cheating spontaneity with pre-programmed tunes, would look like a beautiful slouching monster. The high-voltage orange floodlights would shine through a cloud of winged insects and onto the waiting crowd (if ten people make a crowd), exposing eyebrows choreographed in a beautiful dance of perplexity, hands turning blue around cold glasses fizzing with cold drinks. A couple of people would speak into their cell phones. Then the police would arrive in jeeps and drive them all away.

The flyovers were passé. It was the Delhi Metro—appearing overnight as a series of giant digs through Delhi's spinal tract, mounds of earth shoveled handsomely and packed onto unused sidewalks—that people now pined for.

The Flyover Yaars were all image and little singing.

So, in a sense, things had been going well for Arjun when the disaster happened.

This was the start of the disaster: in September, Mrs. Ahuja went into labor and was rushed to the hospital and Arjun didn't even know. Mrs. Ahuja gave birth to a healthy baby girl, the fourteenth and (for a while) the last of the Ahujas and the whole time Arjun was unreachable on his cell phone—why? Because he was doing an important political favor for his father, which involved buying seventy boxes of sweetmeats for supporters and not answering calls from random numbers. He came home and was surprised to find only servants and five of his siblings, each of whom told him the same thing: *Where were you, bhaiya?*

He had never missed any of Mama's frequent births, and he hadn't intended to miss this one. But even this oversight could have been excused. A birth lasts a few hours; what counts is the aftermath. Except when Arjun saw Mama lying on a stretcher in the hospital, he didn't know what to say to her. He saw her and kissed her on the cheek and cooed politely with the curled-up puckered little baby girl that was trying her hardest to blink in the white lights of the hospital but felt, among his siblings and before his mother, like a courteous stranger. A stranger so courteous and so distant that even that initial scalding temptation to tell his siblings *Why are you smirking, I have work to do, you're worse than stepchildren, Papa didn't even want to marry Mama, she just showed up on the wedding day*, and to enter then into an intimate and fierce battle of succession, all twelve brothers and sisters surrounding him like the ordered dials of a clock while he shivered and turned endlessly within the scope of their machinations—a Mahabharat for modern times—was now gone.

He was neutral territory. He was a disaster of indifference.

Mrs. Ahuja could tell. She reclined on the bed and looked at Arjun and remembered her first time in the hospital—when she had given birth to Varun. She had held Varun to her breast and nursed him, her eyes on four-year-old Arjun as he sat on a little rotating stool and cranked himself up toward her. He didn't want a new brother. He had stuck his tongue out at Sangita. Behind Arjun, the steel and the white sheets of the hospital had reminded Sangita of snow, Dalhousie in winter, how once she had put her hand on a lamppost on the roadside and felt a cold so furious and blue it might as well have been shock. Only then, she had had the tight, gloved hand of her mother to retreat into.

Rakesh had provided no such comfort; years later, only Arjun had.

He was smiling shyly at her now, but Sangita said nothing. Deep in the burgeoning mess of her hair was a zigzag of metal, a hairpin that the doctor had forgotten to confiscate before they robed her in green overalls. She reached for that geometric hardness, pulled it out, let it tumble through the freed vines of her hair. The hairpin hit the ground at the same time that Arjun bent down to find it, his knees now on the floor, hands raking the dust, peering under the bed. She straightened up on the rail and watched him from above as he came up from the floor with the same earnest gaze as his father, that handsome face of worry, and she knew once and for all that she had lost her son.

Yet—maybe it was the relief of birth or just her growing resilience or the fact that she was excited by the prospect of hordes of people descending on her with congratulations and ladoos and looks of distant admiration reserved for geniuses (*put her in a room, and she will produce!*)—she couldn't bring herself to focus on this loss, she could only feel a deep gratefulness for everything, for the children ringed around her, for the fact that she'd survived another pregnancy, for Arjun's presence, howsoever spectral.

She was grateful that she could still see him, still touch him. She was grateful for all the time she'd had with him. She was grateful that he knew what he knew and didn't resent her.

Now if only the same could be said about her dear husband.